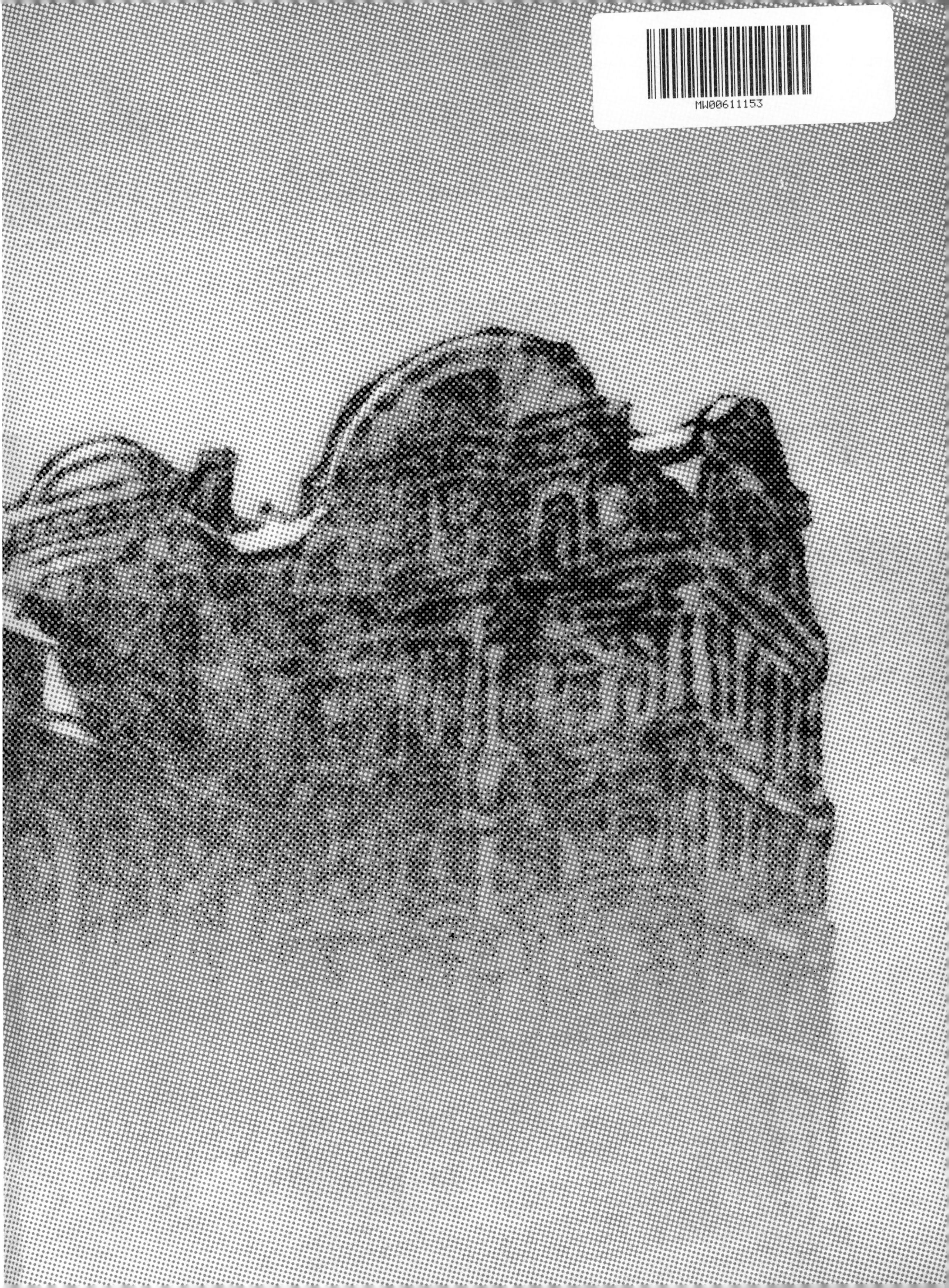

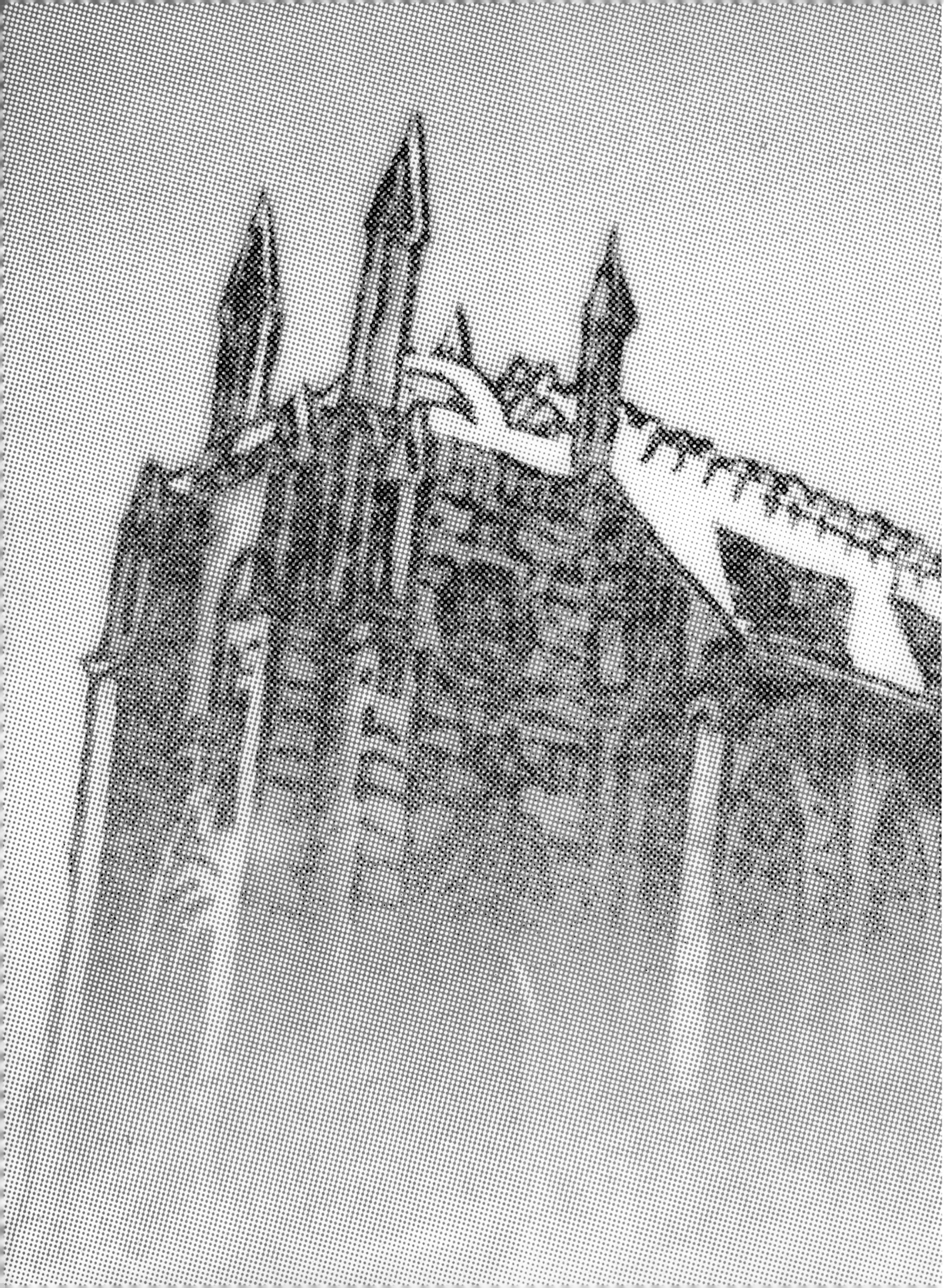

RICHARD CORBEN   RICHARD MARGOPOULOS

EDGAR ALLAN POE'S

THE FALL OF THE HOUSE OF USHER
and other TALES OF TERROR

DEL REY   BALLANTINE BOOKS   NEW YORK

Edgar Allan Poe is a work of fiction. Names, places, and incidents either are a product of the authors' imaginations or are used fictitiously.

2005 Del Rey Books Trade Paperback Edition

Published in the United States by Del Rey Books, an imprint of The Random House Publishing Group, a division of Random House, Inc., New York. Originally published in the United States by Catalan Communications, in 1985.

DEL REY is a registered trademark and the Del Rey colophon is a trademark of Random House, Inc.

This edition published by arrangement with Mame Holdings, LLC.

ISBN 0-345-48313-8

Printed in the United States of America

www.delreybooks.com

9 8 7 6 5 4 3 2 1

PROLOGUE

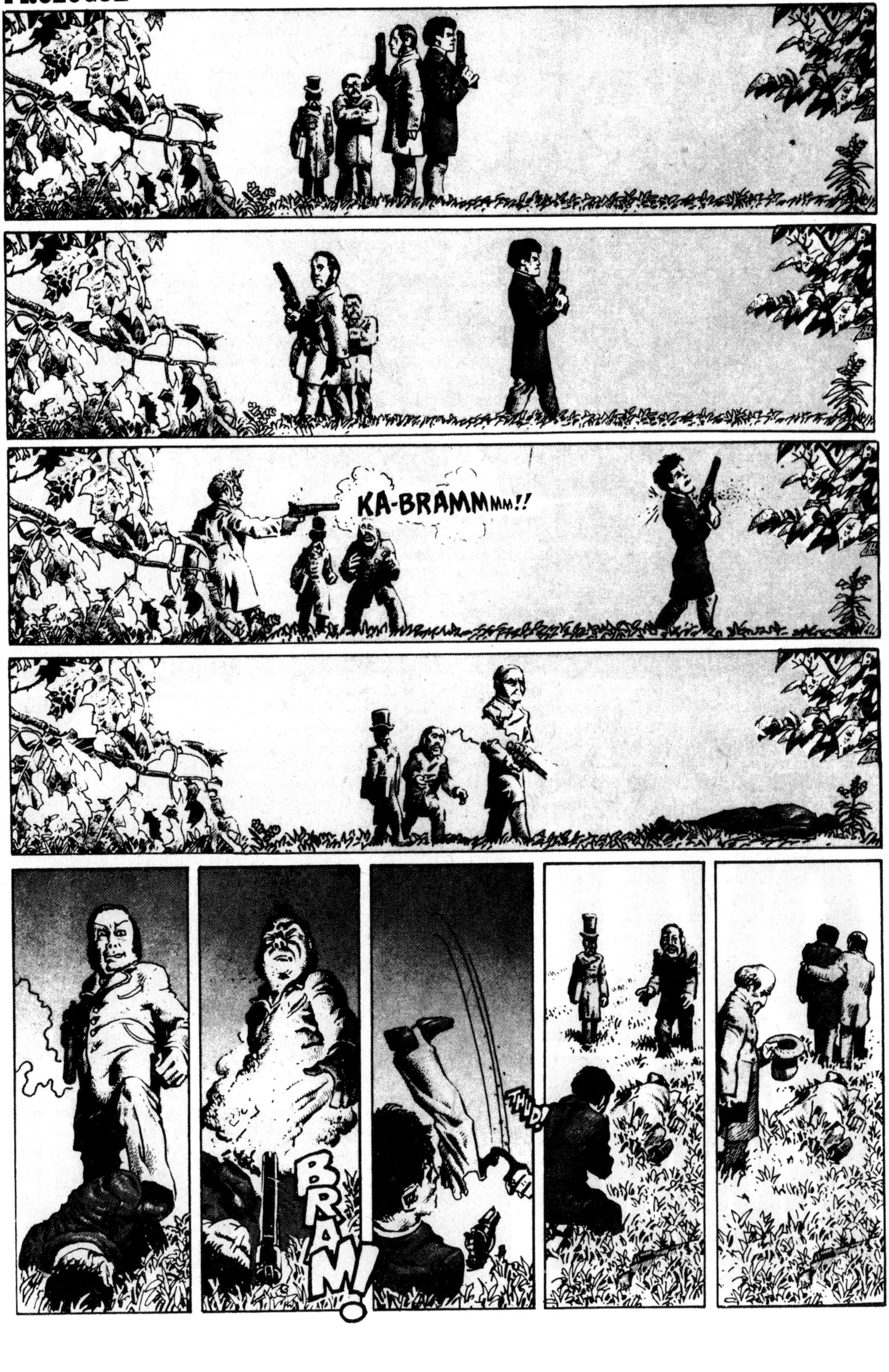
KA-BRAMMMM!!
THUD!
BRAM!

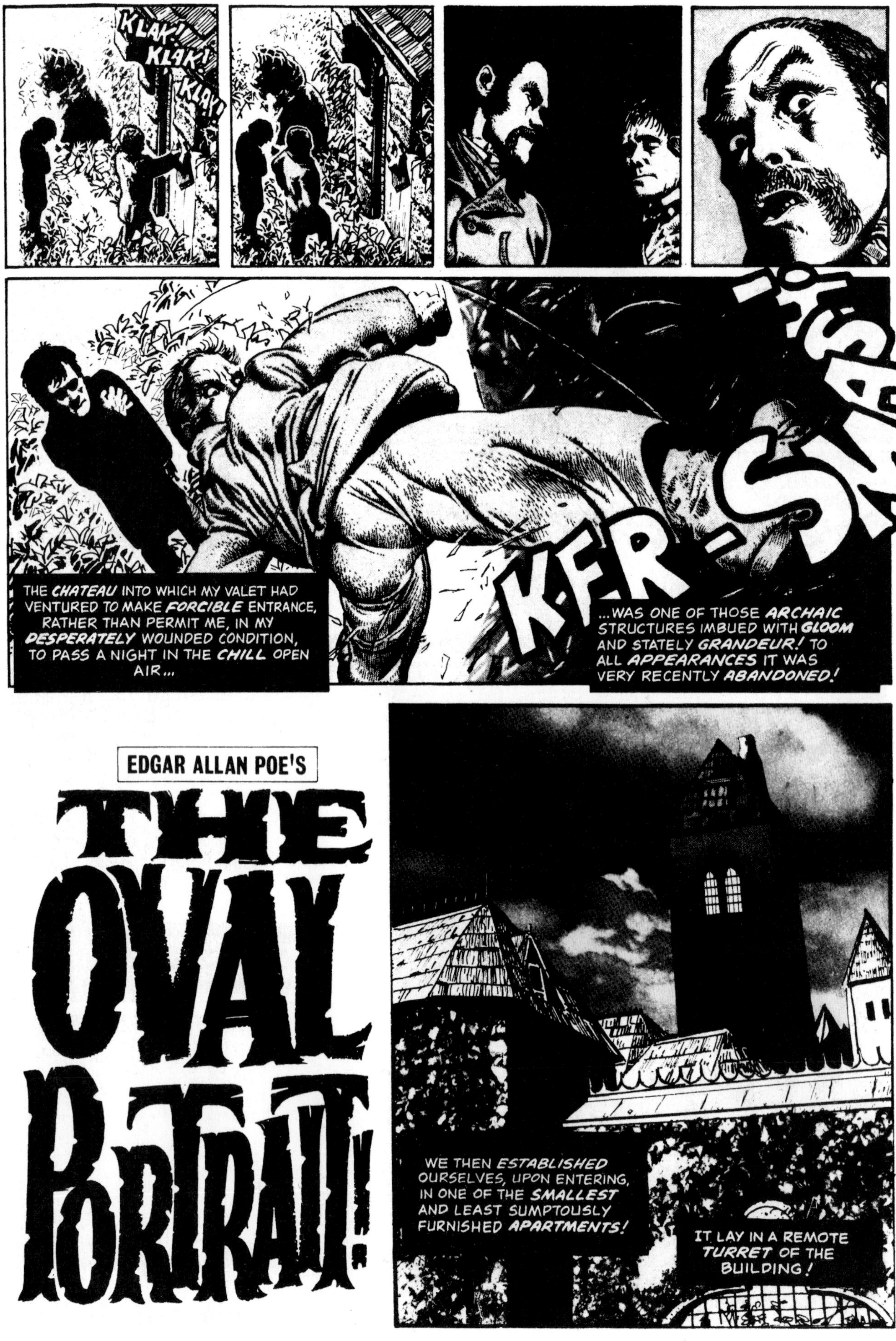
KLAK!
KLAK!
KLAK!
K-FR-SMASH!
THE CHATEAU INTO WHICH MY VALET HAD VENTURED TO MAKE FORCIBLE ENTRANCE, RATHER THAN PERMIT ME, IN MY DESPERATELY WOUNDED CONDITION, TO PASS A NIGHT IN THE CHILL OPEN AIR...
...WAS ONE OF THOSE ARCHAIC STRUCTURES IMBUED WITH GLOOM AND STATELY GRANDEUR! TO ALL APPEARANCES IT WAS VERY RECENTLY ABANDONED!
EDGAR ALLAN POE'S
THE OVAL PORTRAIT!
WE THEN ESTABLISHED OURSELVES, UPON ENTERING, IN ONE OF THE SMALLEST AND LEAST SUMPTOUSLY FURNISHED APARTMENTS!
IT LAY IN A REMOTE TURRET OF THE BUILDING!

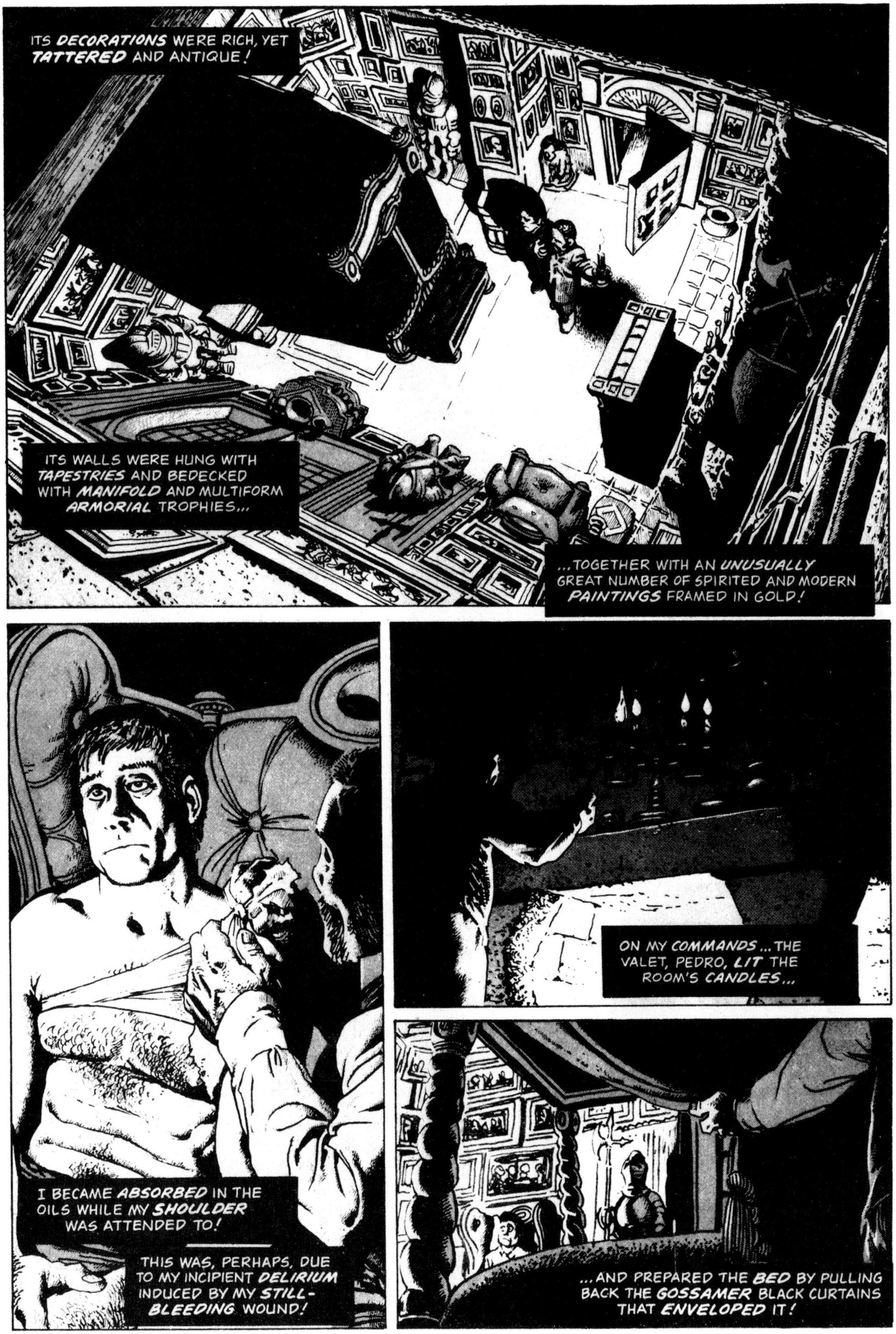
ITS DECORATIONS WERE RICH, YET TATTERED AND ANTIQUE!
ITS WALLS WERE HUNG WITH TAPESTRIES AND BEDECKED WITH MANIFOLD AND MULTIFORM ARMORIAL TROPHIES...
...TOGETHER WITH AN UNUSUALLY GREAT NUMBER OF SPIRITED AND MODERN PAINTINGS FRAMED IN GOLD!
I BECAME ABSORBED IN THE OILS WHILE MY SHOULDER WAS ATTENDED TO!
THIS WAS, PERHAPS, DUE TO MY INCIPIENT DELIRIUM INDUCED BY MY STILL-BLEEDING WOUND!
ON MY COMMANDS... THE VALET, PEDRO, LIT THE ROOM'S CANDLES...
...AND PREPARED THE BED BY PULLING BACK THE GOSSAMER BLACK CURTAINS THAT ENVELOPED IT!

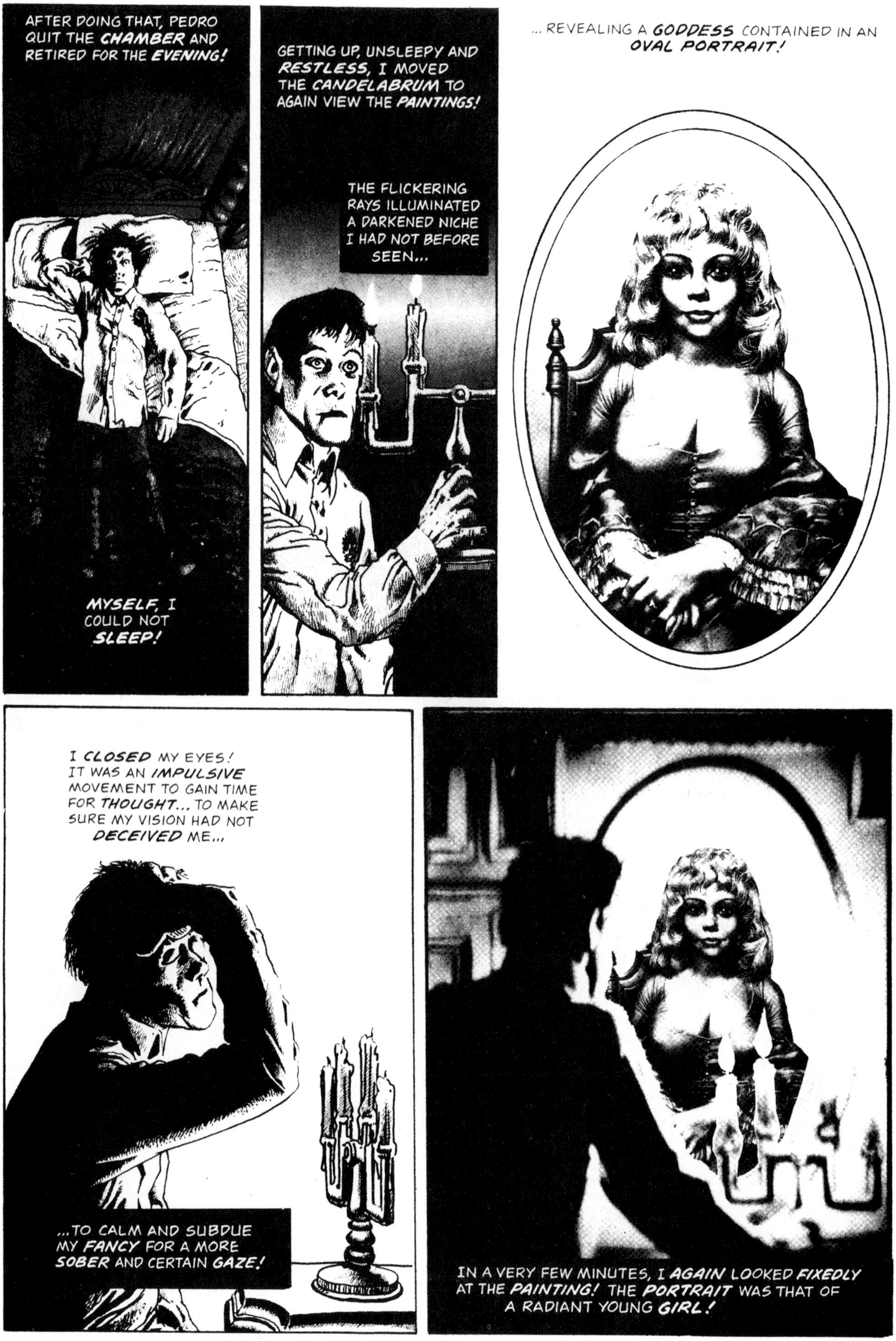
AFTER DOING THAT, PEDRO QUIT THE CHAMBER AND RETIRED FOR THE EVENING!
MYSELF, I COULD NOT SLEEP!
GETTING UP, UNSLEEPY AND RESTLESS, I MOVED THE CANDELABRUM TO AGAIN VIEW THE PAINTINGS!
THE FLICKERING RAYS ILLUMINATED A DARKENED NICHE I HAD NOT BEFORE SEEN...
... REVEALING A GODDESS CONTAINED IN AN OVAL PORTRAIT!
I CLOSED MY EYES! IT WAS AN IMPULSIVE MOVEMENT TO GAIN TIME FOR THOUGHT... TO MAKE SURE MY VISION HAD NOT DECEIVED ME...
...TO CALM AND SUBDUE MY FANCY FOR A MORE SOBER AND CERTAIN GAZE!
IN A VERY FEW MINUTES, I AGAIN LOOKED FIXEDLY AT THE PAINTING! THE PORTRAIT WAS THAT OF A RADIANT YOUNG GIRL!

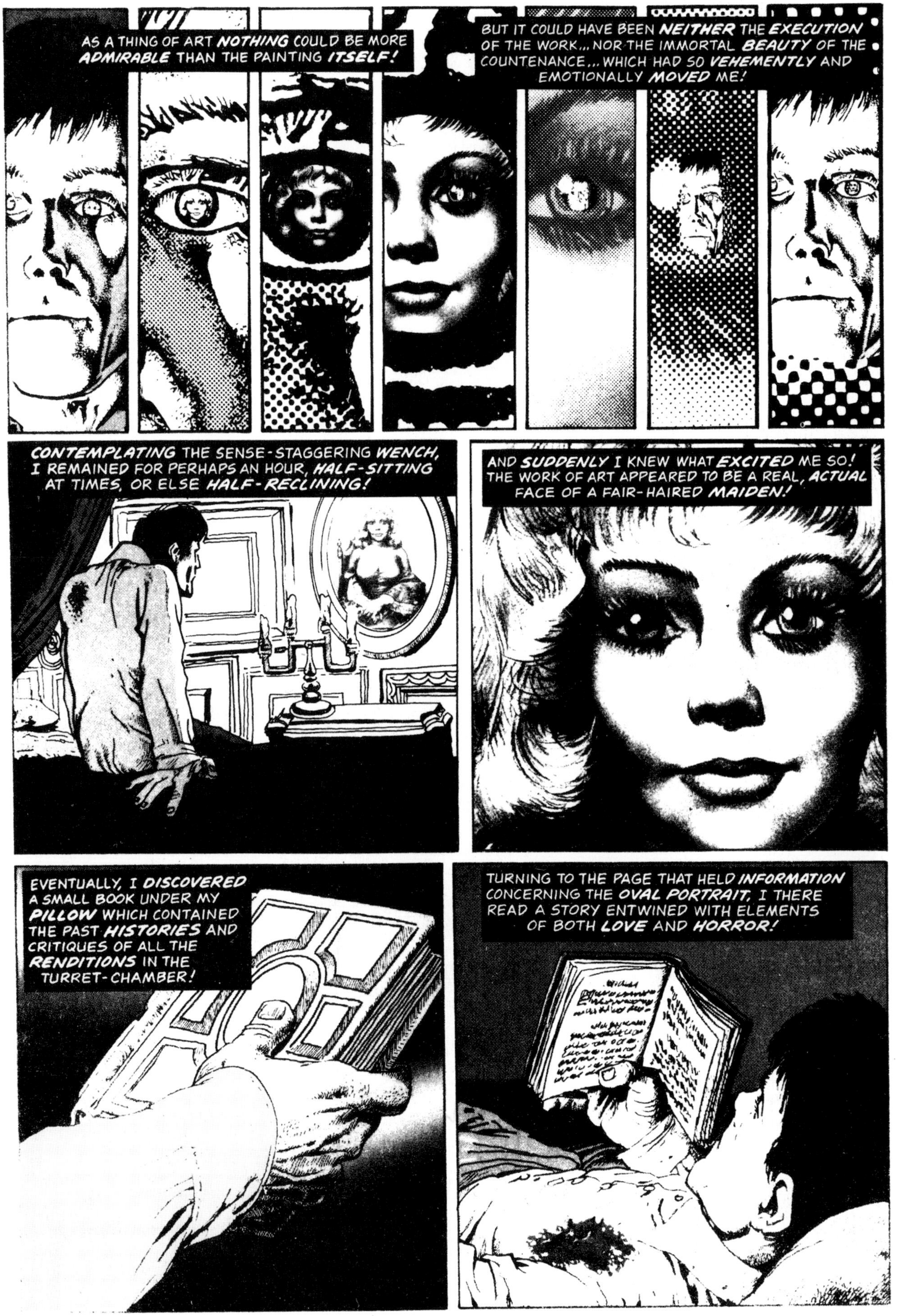
AS A THING OF ART NOTHING COULD BE MORE ADMIRABLE THAN THE PAINTING ITSELF!
BUT IT COULD HAVE BEEN NEITHER THE EXECUTION OF THE WORK... NOR THE IMMORTAL BEAUTY OF THE COUNTENANCE... WHICH HAD SO VEHEMENTLY AND EMOTIONALLY MOVED ME!
CONTEMPLATING THE SENSE-STAGGERING WENCH, I REMAINED FOR PERHAPS AN HOUR, HALF-SITTING AT TIMES, OR ELSE HALF-RECLINING!
AND SUDDENLY I KNEW WHAT EXCITED ME SO! THE WORK OF ART APPEARED TO BE A REAL, ACTUAL FACE OF A FAIR-HAIRED MAIDEN!
EVENTUALLY, I DISCOVERED A SMALL BOOK UNDER MY PILLOW WHICH CONTAINED THE PAST HISTORIES AND CRITIQUES OF ALL THE RENDITIONS IN THE TURRET-CHAMBER!
TURNING TO THE PAGE THAT HELD INFORMATION CONCERNING THE OVAL PORTRAIT, I THERE READ A STORY ENTWINED WITH ELEMENTS OF BOTH LOVE AND HORROR!

SHE WAS A WENCH OF **RAREST** BEAUTY, AND NOT MORE **LOVELY** THAN FULL OF **GLEE!**

AND **EVIL** WAS THE HOUR SHE **SAW**, AND **LOVED**, AND **WEDDED** THE PAINTER!

HE, PASSIONATE, STUDIOUS, **AUSTERE**... AND ALREADY HAVING A **BRIDE** IN HIS **ART**...

...SHE A MAIDEN, ALL **LIGHT** AND SMILES, AND **FROLICKSOME** AS THE YOUNG **FAWN**...

...**LOVING** AND CHERISHING ALL **THINGS**... **ESPECIALLY** HER BELOVED **HUSBAND**...

...**HATING** ONLY THE **ART** WHICH WAS HER **RIVAL**...**DREADING** ONLY THE PALLET AND BRUSHES AND OTHER **UNTOWARD** INSTRUMENTS WHICH **DEPRIVED** HER OF HER **LOVER!**

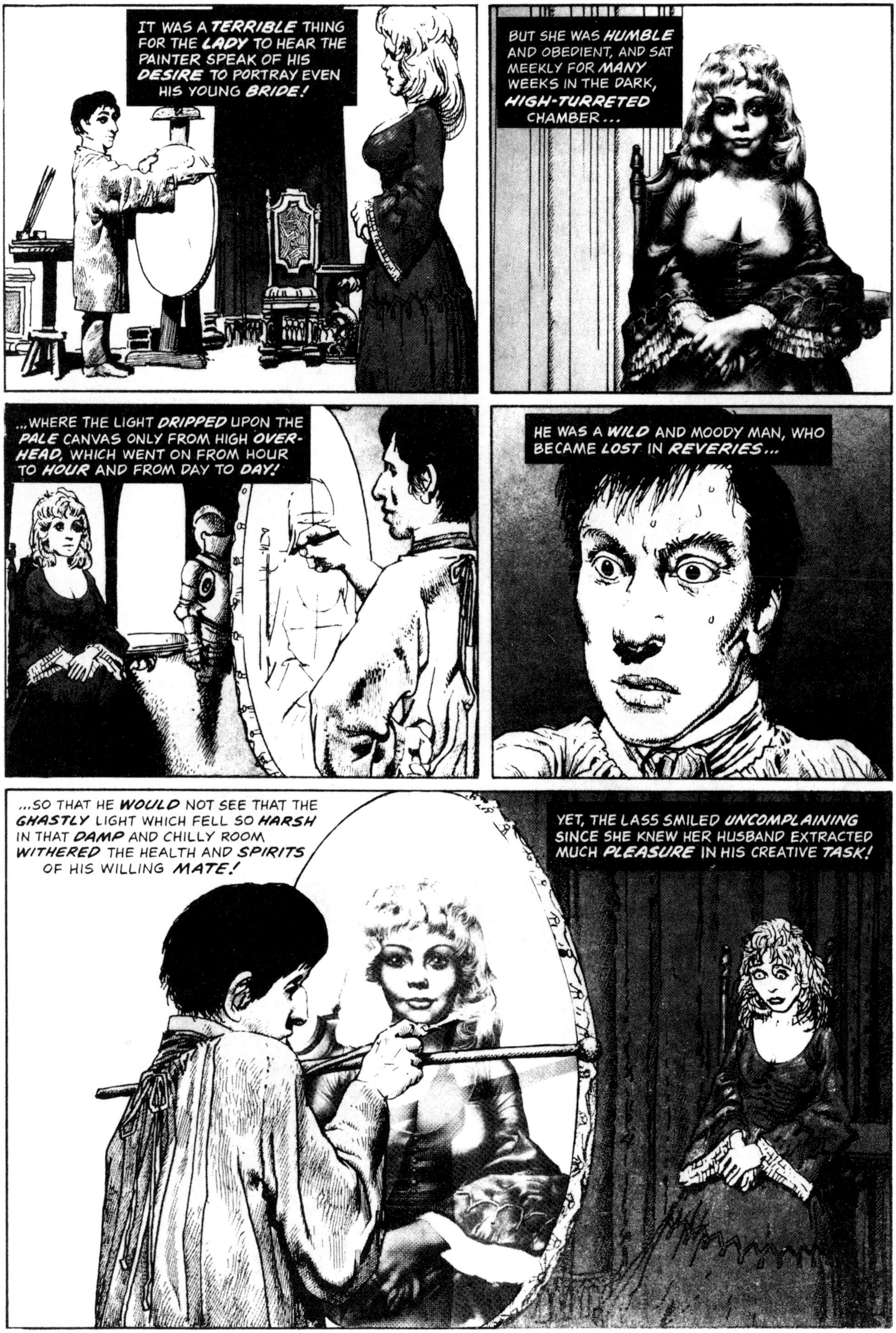
IT WAS A TERRIBLE THING FOR THE LADY TO HEAR THE PAINTER SPEAK OF HIS DESIRE TO PORTRAY EVEN HIS YOUNG BRIDE!
BUT SHE WAS HUMBLE AND OBEDIENT, AND SAT MEEKLY FOR MANY WEEKS IN THE DARK, HIGH-TURRETED CHAMBER...
...WHERE THE LIGHT DRIPPED UPON THE PALE CANVAS ONLY FROM HIGH OVERHEAD, WHICH WENT ON FROM HOUR TO HOUR AND FROM DAY TO DAY!
HE WAS A WILD AND MOODY MAN, WHO BECAME LOST IN REVERIES...
...SO THAT HE WOULD NOT SEE THAT THE GHASTLY LIGHT WHICH FELL SO HARSH IN THAT DAMP AND CHILLY ROOM WITHERED THE HEALTH AND SPIRITS OF HIS WILLING MATE!
YET, THE LASS SMILED UNCOMPLAINING SINCE SHE KNEW HER HUSBAND EXTRACTED MUCH PLEASURE IN HIS CREATIVE TASK!

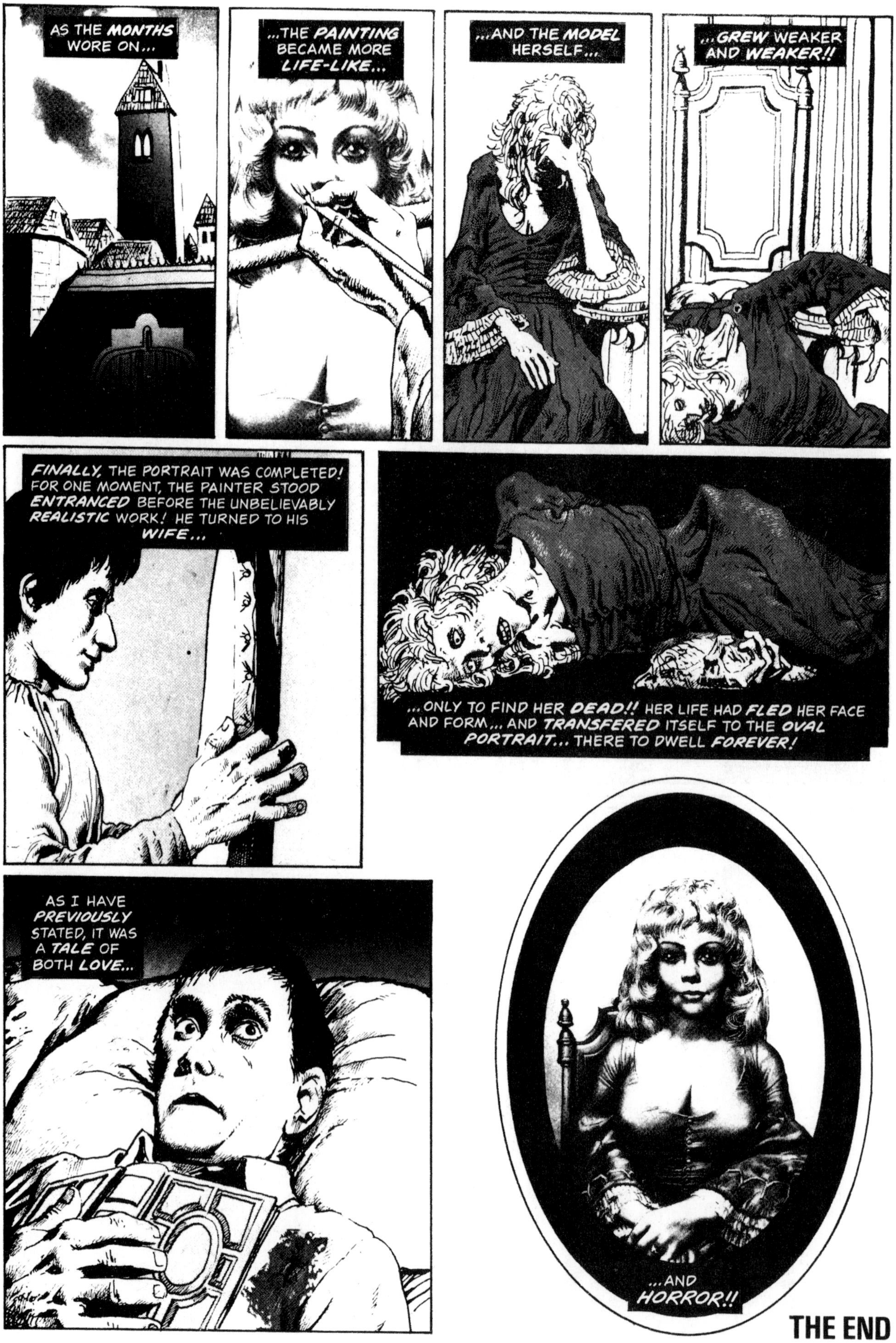
AS THE MONTHS WORE ON...
...THE PAINTING BECAME MORE LIFE-LIKE...
...AND THE MODEL HERSELF...
...GREW WEAKER AND WEAKER!!
FINALLY, THE PORTRAIT WAS COMPLETED! FOR ONE MOMENT, THE PAINTER STOOD ENTRANCED BEFORE THE UNBELIEVABLY REALISTIC WORK! HE TURNED TO HIS WIFE...
...ONLY TO FIND HER DEAD!! HER LIFE HAD FLED HER FACE AND FORM... AND TRANSFERED ITSELF TO THE OVAL PORTRAIT... THERE TO DWELL FOREVER!
AS I HAVE PREVIOUSLY STATED, IT WAS A TALE OF BOTH LOVE...
...AND HORROR!!

THE END

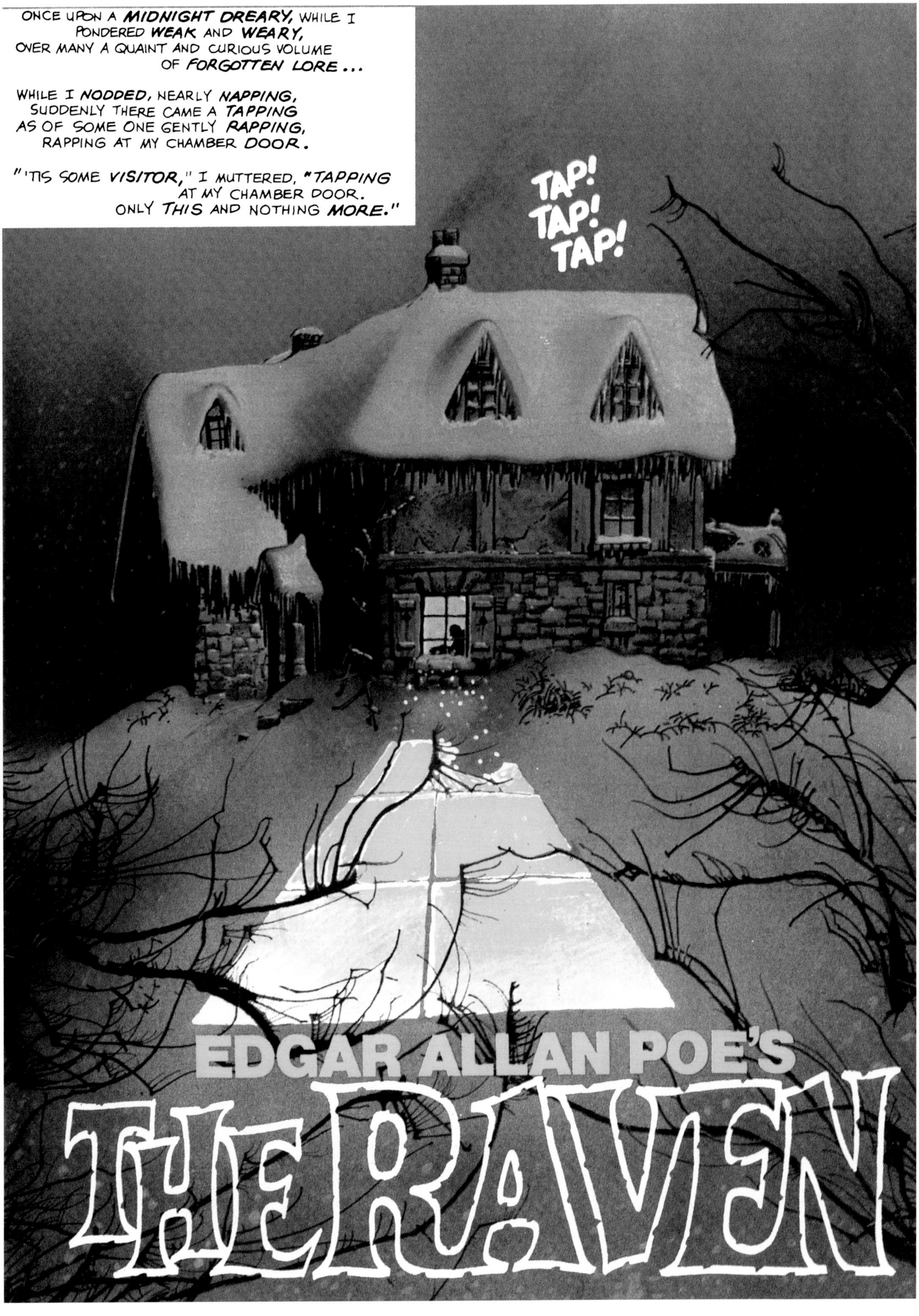
ONCE UPON A MIDNIGHT DREARY, WHILE I PONDERED WEAK AND WEARY, OVER MANY A QUAINT AND CURIOUS VOLUME OF FORGOTTEN LORE...
WHILE I NODDED, NEARLY NAPPING, SUDDENLY THERE CAME A TAPPING AS OF SOME ONE GENTLY RAPPING, RAPPING AT MY CHAMBER DOOR.
"'TIS SOME VISITOR," I MUTTERED, "TAPPING AT MY CHAMBER DOOR. ONLY THIS AND NOTHING MORE."
TAP! TAP! TAP!
EDGAR ALLAN POE'S
THE RAVEN

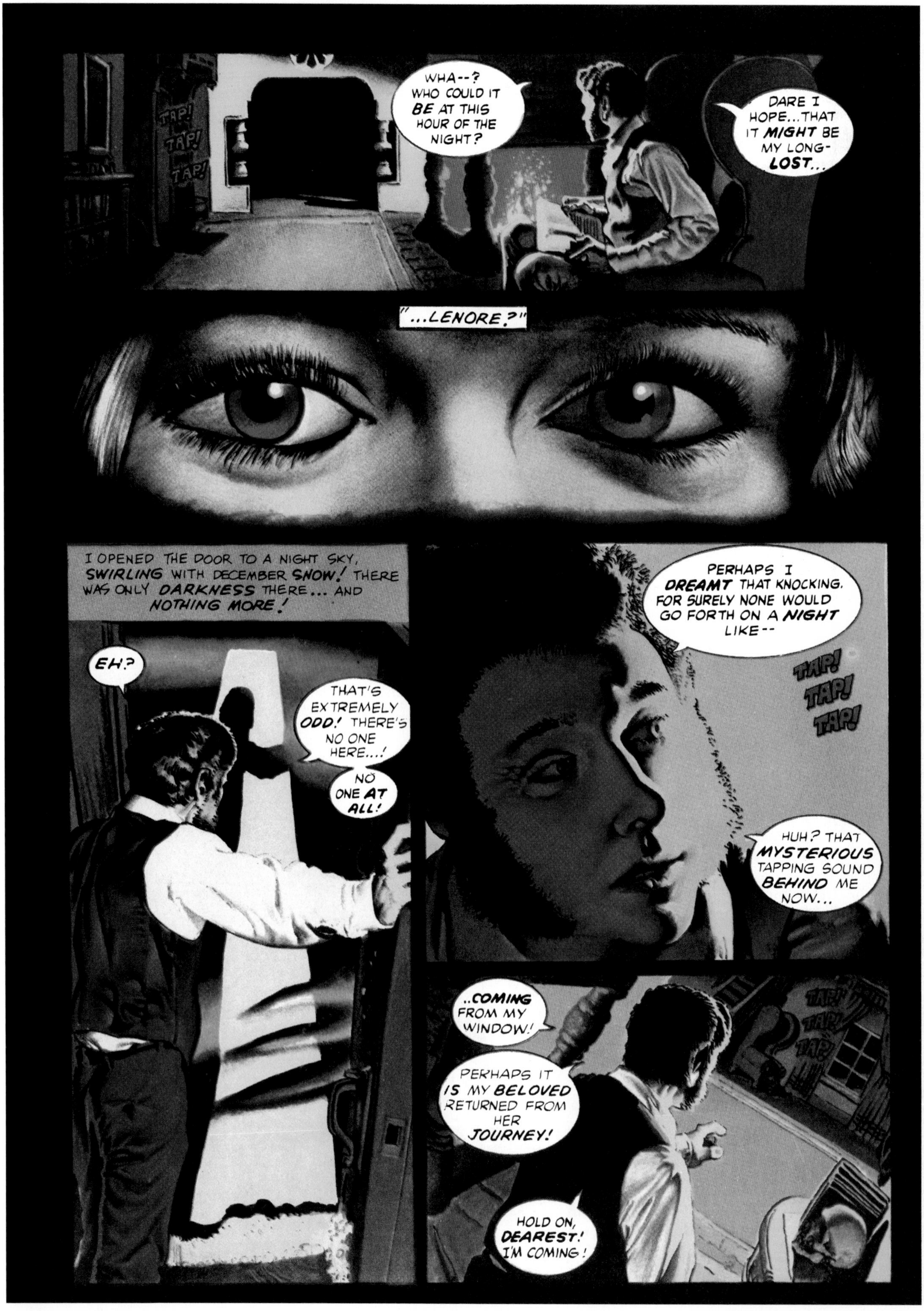
TAP! TAP! TAP!
WHA--? WHO COULD IT BE AT THIS HOUR OF THE NIGHT?
DARE I HOPE...THAT IT MIGHT BE MY LONG-LOST...
"...LENORE?"
I OPENED THE DOOR TO A NIGHT SKY, SWIRLING WITH DECEMBER SNOW! THERE WAS ONLY DARKNESS THERE... AND NOTHING MORE!
EH?
THAT'S EXTREMELY ODD! THERE'S NO ONE HERE...!
NO ONE AT ALL!
PERHAPS I DREAMT THAT KNOCKING. FOR SURELY NONE WOULD GO FORTH ON A NIGHT LIKE--
TAP! TAP! TAP!
HUH? THAT MYSTERIOUS TAPPING SOUND BEHIND ME NOW...
..COMING FROM MY WINDOW!
TAP! TAP! TAP!
PERHAPS IT IS MY BELOVED RETURNED FROM HER JOURNEY!
HOLD ON, DEAREST! I'M COMING!

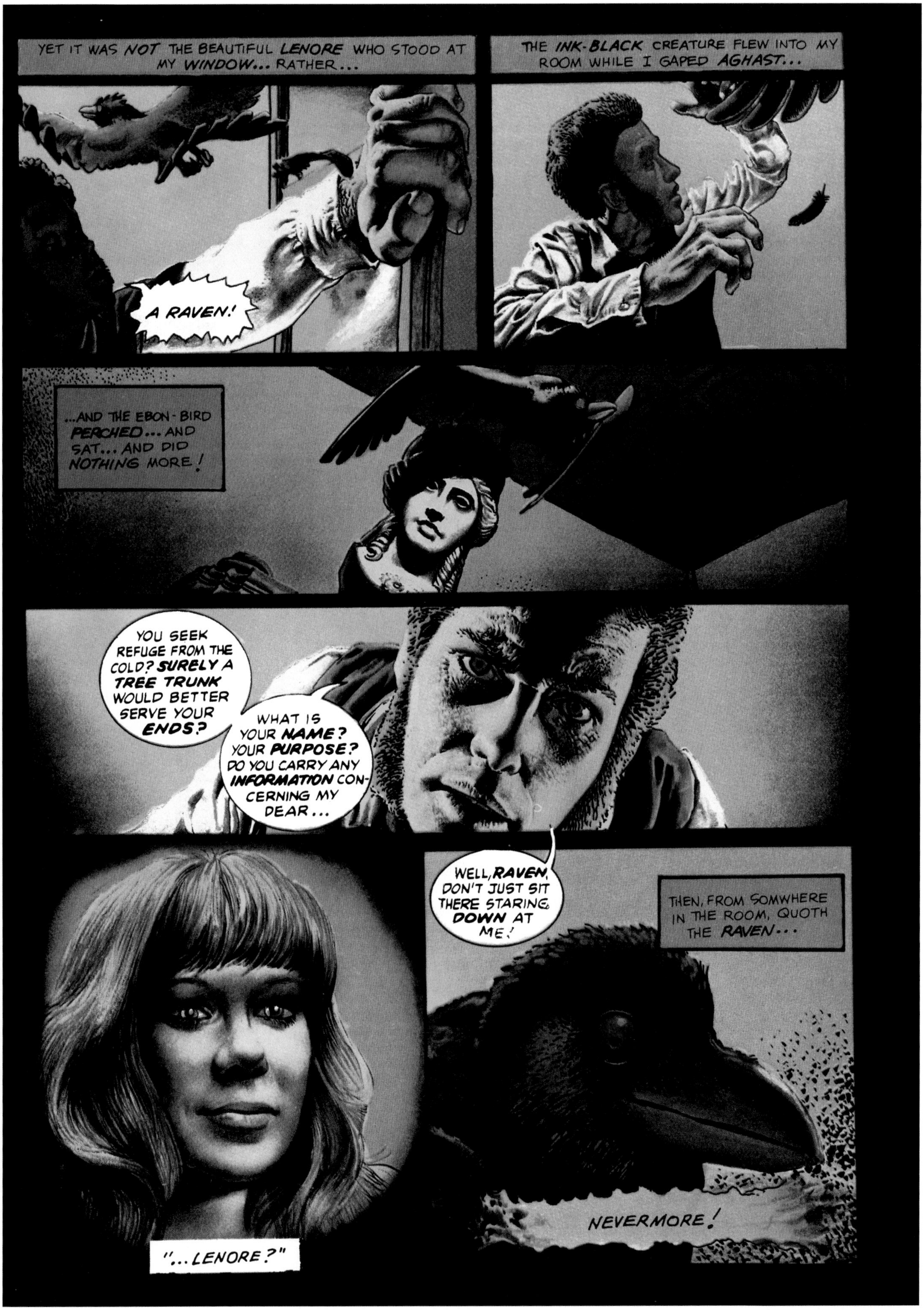
YET IT WAS NOT THE BEAUTIFUL LENORE WHO STOOD AT MY WINDOW... RATHER...
A RAVEN!
THE INK-BLACK CREATURE FLEW INTO MY ROOM WHILE I GAPED AGHAST...
...AND THE EBON-BIRD PERCHED... AND SAT... AND DID NOTHING MORE!
YOU SEEK REFUGE FROM THE COLD? SURELY A TREE TRUNK WOULD BETTER SERVE YOUR ENDS?
WHAT IS YOUR NAME? YOUR PURPOSE? DO YOU CARRY ANY INFORMATION CONCERNING MY DEAR...
"...LENORE?"
WELL, RAVEN, DON'T JUST SIT THERE STARING DOWN AT ME!
THEN, FROM SOMWHERE IN THE ROOM, QUOTH THE RAVEN...
NEVERMORE!

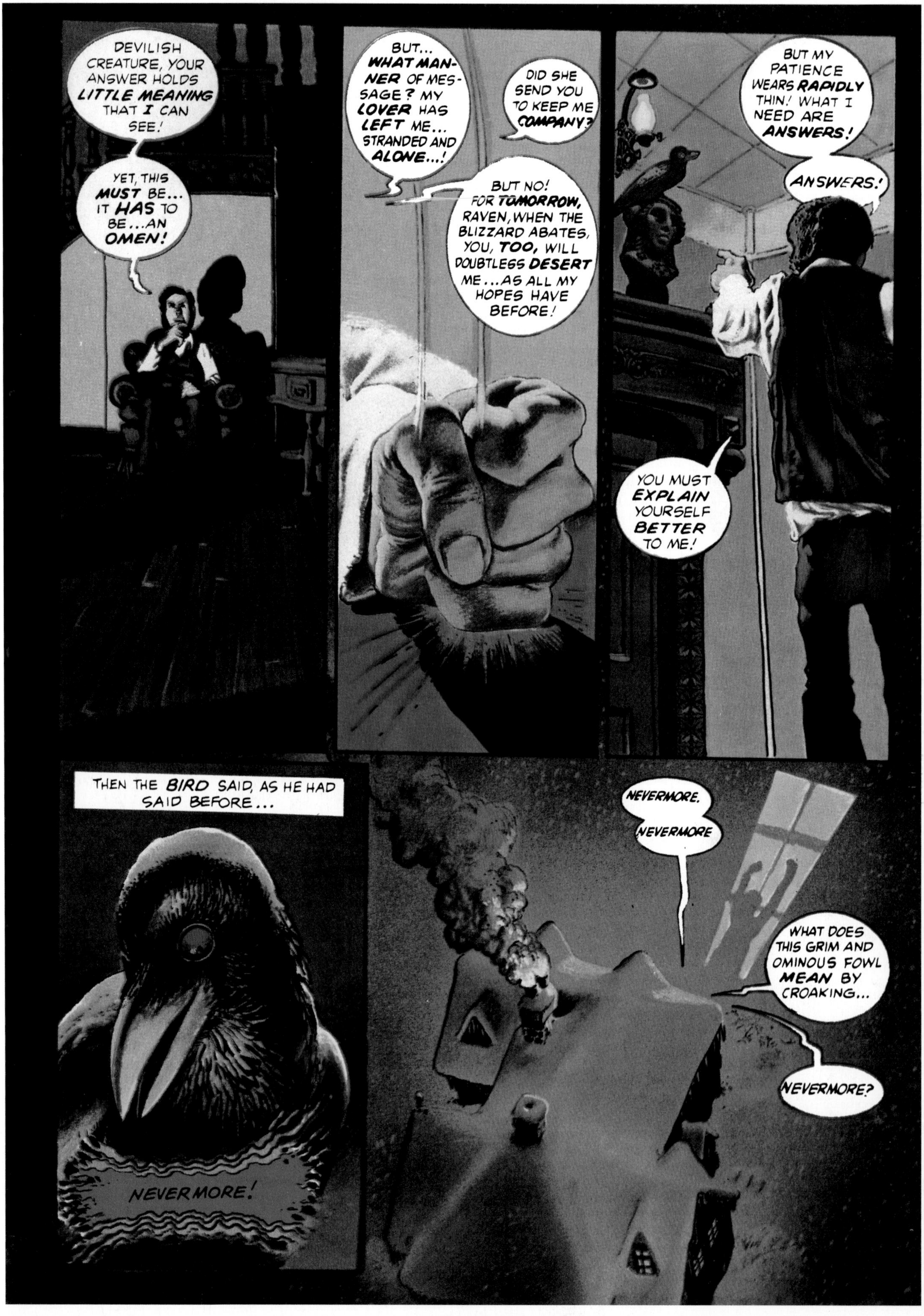
DEVILISH CREATURE, YOUR ANSWER HOLDS LITTLE MEANING THAT I CAN SEE!
YET, THIS MUST BE... IT HAS TO BE...AN OMEN!
BUT... WHAT MANNER OF MESSAGE? MY LOVER HAS LEFT ME... STRANDED AND ALONE...!
DID SHE SEND YOU TO KEEP ME COMPANY?
BUT NO! FOR TOMORROW, RAVEN, WHEN THE BLIZZARD ABATES, YOU, TOO, WILL DOUBTLESS DESERT ME...AS ALL MY HOPES HAVE BEFORE!
BUT MY PATIENCE WEARS RAPIDLY THIN! WHAT I NEED ARE ANSWERS!
ANSWERS!
YOU MUST EXPLAIN YOURSELF BETTER TO ME!
THEN THE BIRD SAID, AS HE HAD SAID BEFORE...
NEVERMORE!
NEVERMORE.
NEVERMORE
WHAT DOES THIS GRIM AND OMINOUS FOWL MEAN BY CROAKING...
NEVERMORE?

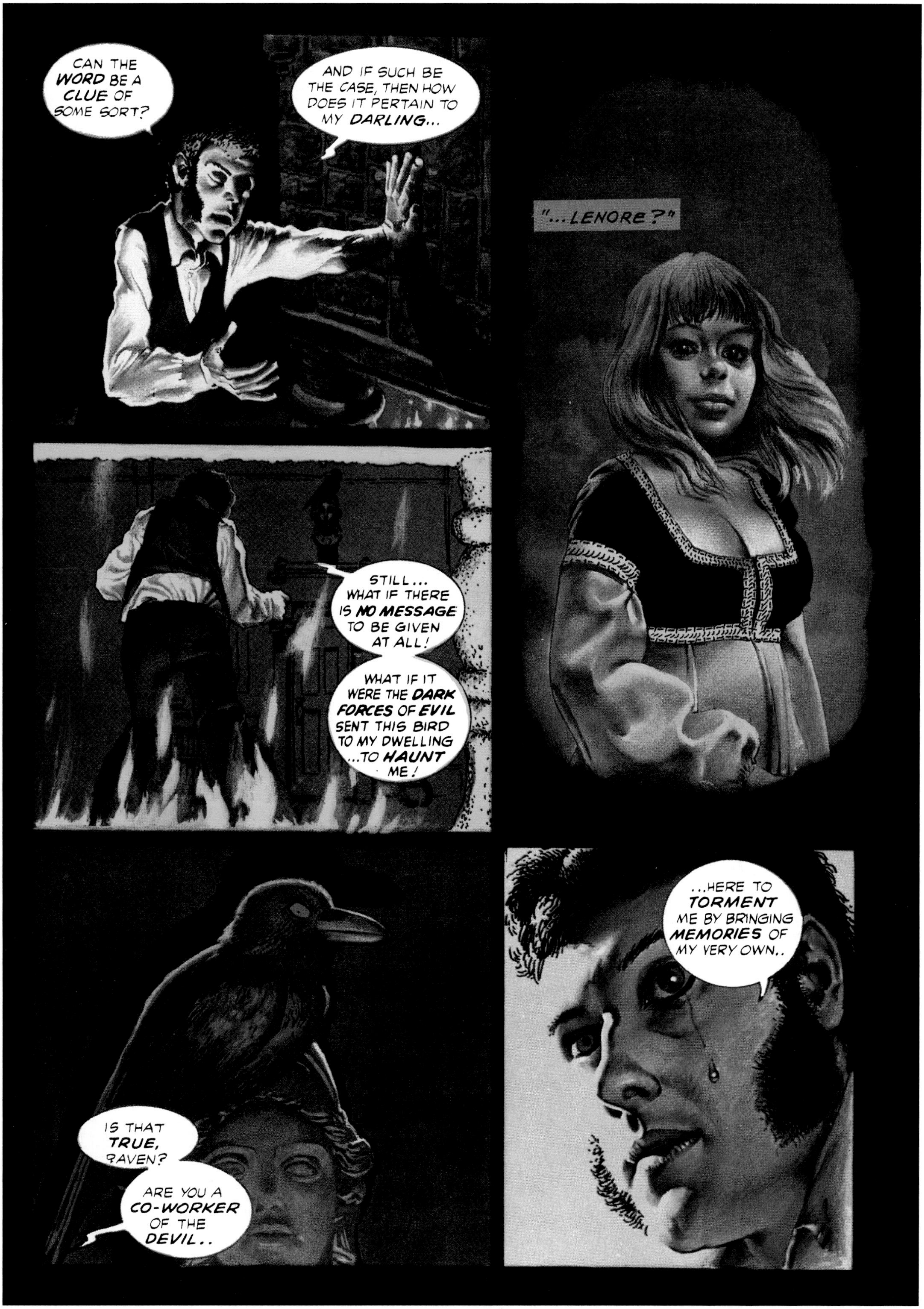
CAN THE WORD BE A CLUE OF SOME SORT?
AND IF SUCH BE THE CASE, THEN HOW DOES IT PERTAIN TO MY DARLING...
"...LENORE?"
STILL... WHAT IF THERE IS NO MESSAGE TO BE GIVEN AT ALL!
WHAT IF IT WERE THE DARK FORCES OF EVIL SENT THIS BIRD TO MY DWELLING ...TO HAUNT ME!
IS THAT TRUE, RAVEN?
ARE YOU A CO-WORKER OF THE DEVIL..
...HERE TO TORMENT ME BY BRINGING MEMORIES OF MY VERY OWN..

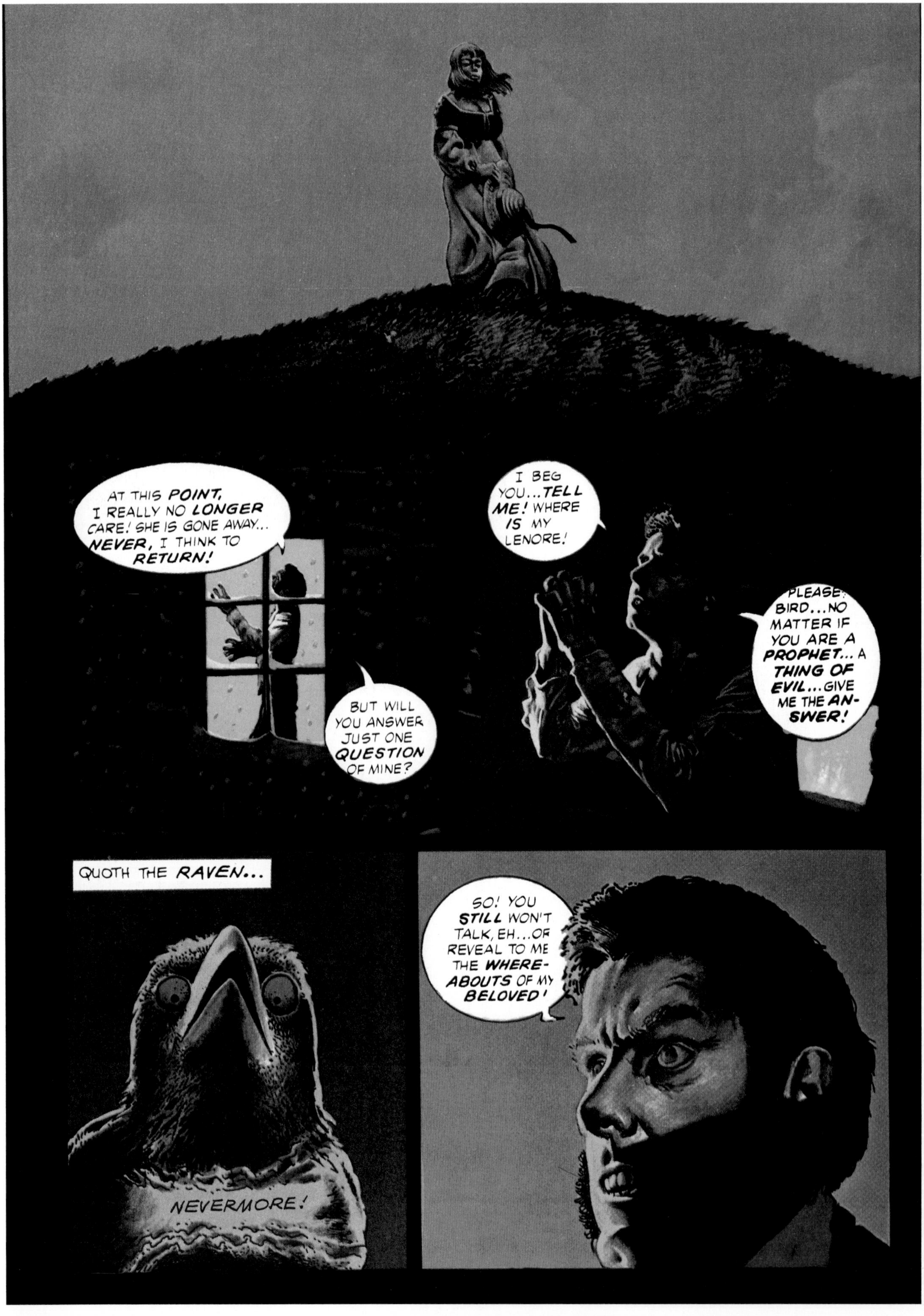
AT THIS POINT, I REALLY NO LONGER CARE! SHE IS GONE AWAY... NEVER, I THINK TO RETURN!
I BEG YOU...TELL ME! WHERE IS MY LENORE!
BUT WILL YOU ANSWER JUST ONE QUESTION OF MINE?
PLEASE! BIRD...NO MATTER IF YOU ARE A PROPHET... A THING OF EVIL...GIVE ME THE AN-SWER!
QUOTH THE RAVEN...
NEVERMORE!
SO! YOU STILL WON'T TALK, EH...OR REVEAL TO ME THE WHERE-ABOUTS OF MY BELOVED!

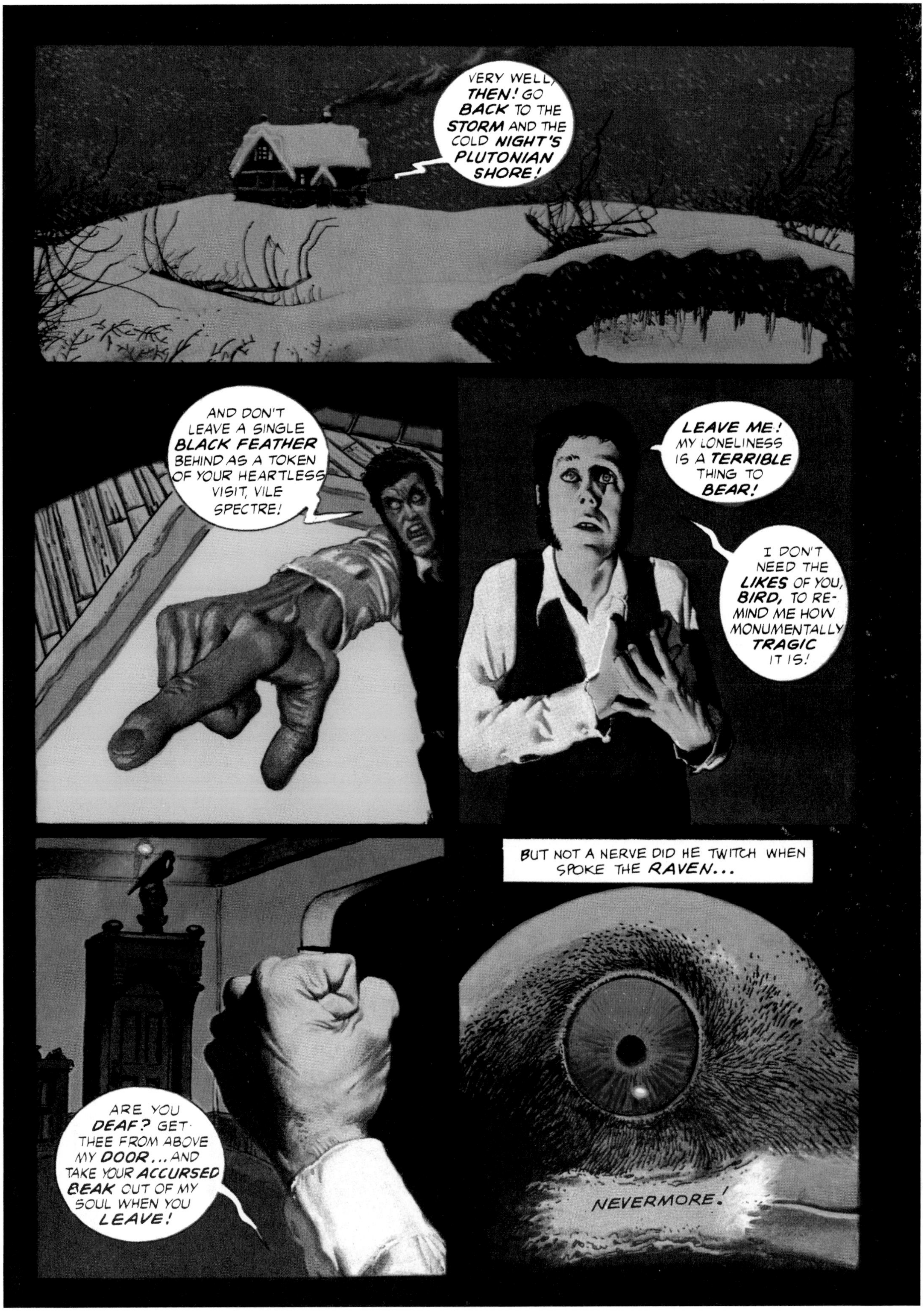
VERY WELL, THEN! GO BACK TO THE STORM AND THE COLD NIGHT'S PLUTONIAN SHORE!
AND DON'T LEAVE A SINGLE BLACK FEATHER BEHIND AS A TOKEN OF YOUR HEARTLESS VISIT, VILE SPECTRE!
LEAVE ME! MY LONELINESS IS A TERRIBLE THING TO BEAR!
I DON'T NEED THE LIKES OF YOU, BIRD, TO RE-MIND ME HOW MONUMENTALLY TRAGIC IT IS!
ARE YOU DEAF? GET THEE FROM ABOVE MY DOOR... AND TAKE YOUR ACCURSED BEAK OUT OF MY SOUL WHEN YOU LEAVE!
BUT NOT A NERVE DID HE TWITCH WHEN SPOKE THE RAVEN...
NEVERMORE!

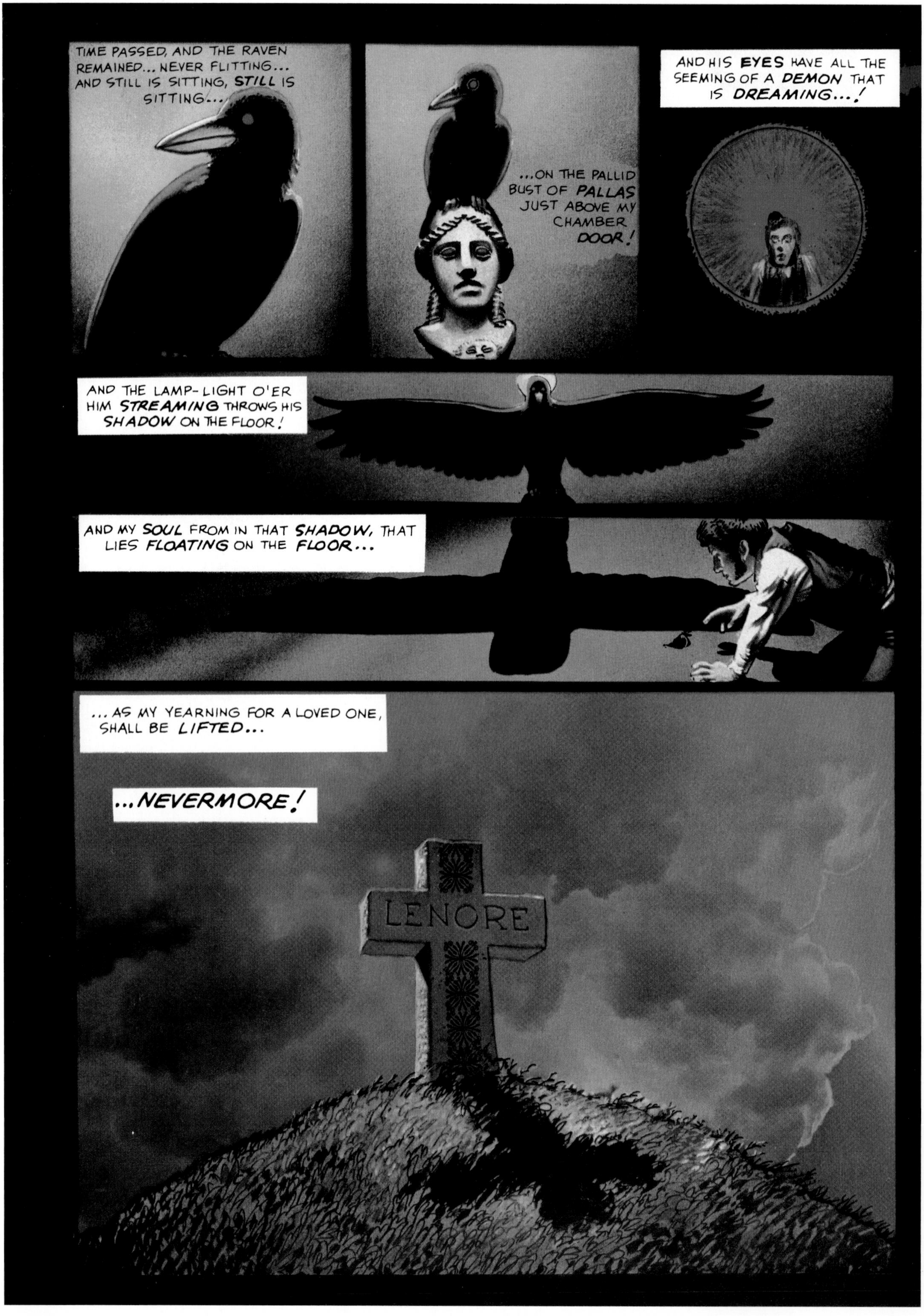
TIME PASSED, AND THE RAVEN REMAINED... NEVER FLITTING... AND STILL IS SITTING, STILL IS SITTING...
...ON THE PALLID BUST OF PALLAS JUST ABOVE MY CHAMBER DOOR!
AND HIS EYES HAVE ALL THE SEEMING OF A DEMON THAT IS DREAMING...!
AND THE LAMP-LIGHT O'ER HIM STREAMING THROWS HIS SHADOW ON THE FLOOR!
AND MY SOUL FROM IN THAT SHADOW, THAT LIES FLOATING ON THE FLOOR...
...AS MY YEARNING FOR A LOVED ONE, SHALL BE LIFTED...
...NEVERMORE!
LENORE

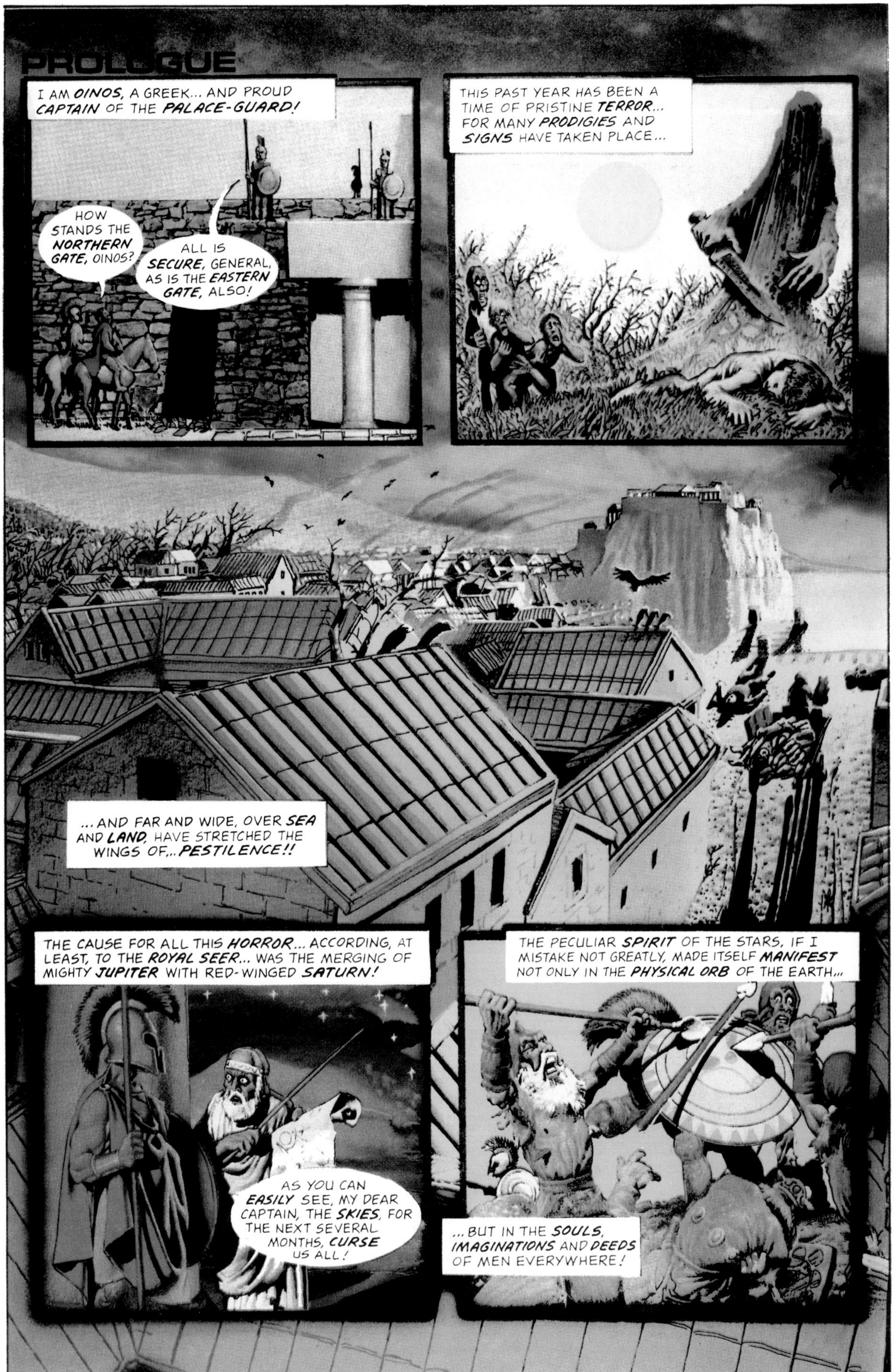
PROLOGUE
I AM OINOS, A GREEK... AND PROUD CAPTAIN OF THE PALACE-GUARD!
HOW STANDS THE NORTHERN GATE, OINOS?
ALL IS SECURE, GENERAL, AS IS THE EASTERN GATE, ALSO!
THIS PAST YEAR HAS BEEN A TIME OF PRISTINE TERROR... FOR MANY PRODIGIES AND SIGNS HAVE TAKEN PLACE...
...AND FAR AND WIDE, OVER SEA AND LAND, HAVE STRETCHED THE WINGS OF... PESTILENCE!!
THE CAUSE FOR ALL THIS HORROR... ACCORDING, AT LEAST, TO THE ROYAL SEER... WAS THE MERGING OF MIGHTY JUPITER WITH RED-WINGED SATURN!
AS YOU CAN EASILY SEE, MY DEAR CAPTAIN, THE SKIES, FOR THE NEXT SEVERAL MONTHS, CURSE US ALL!
THE PECULIAR SPIRIT OF THE STARS, IF I MISTAKE NOT GREATLY, MADE ITSELF MANIFEST NOT ONLY IN THE PHYSICAL ORB OF THE EARTH...
...BUT IN THE SOULS, IMAGINATIONS AND DEEDS OF MEN EVERYWHERE!

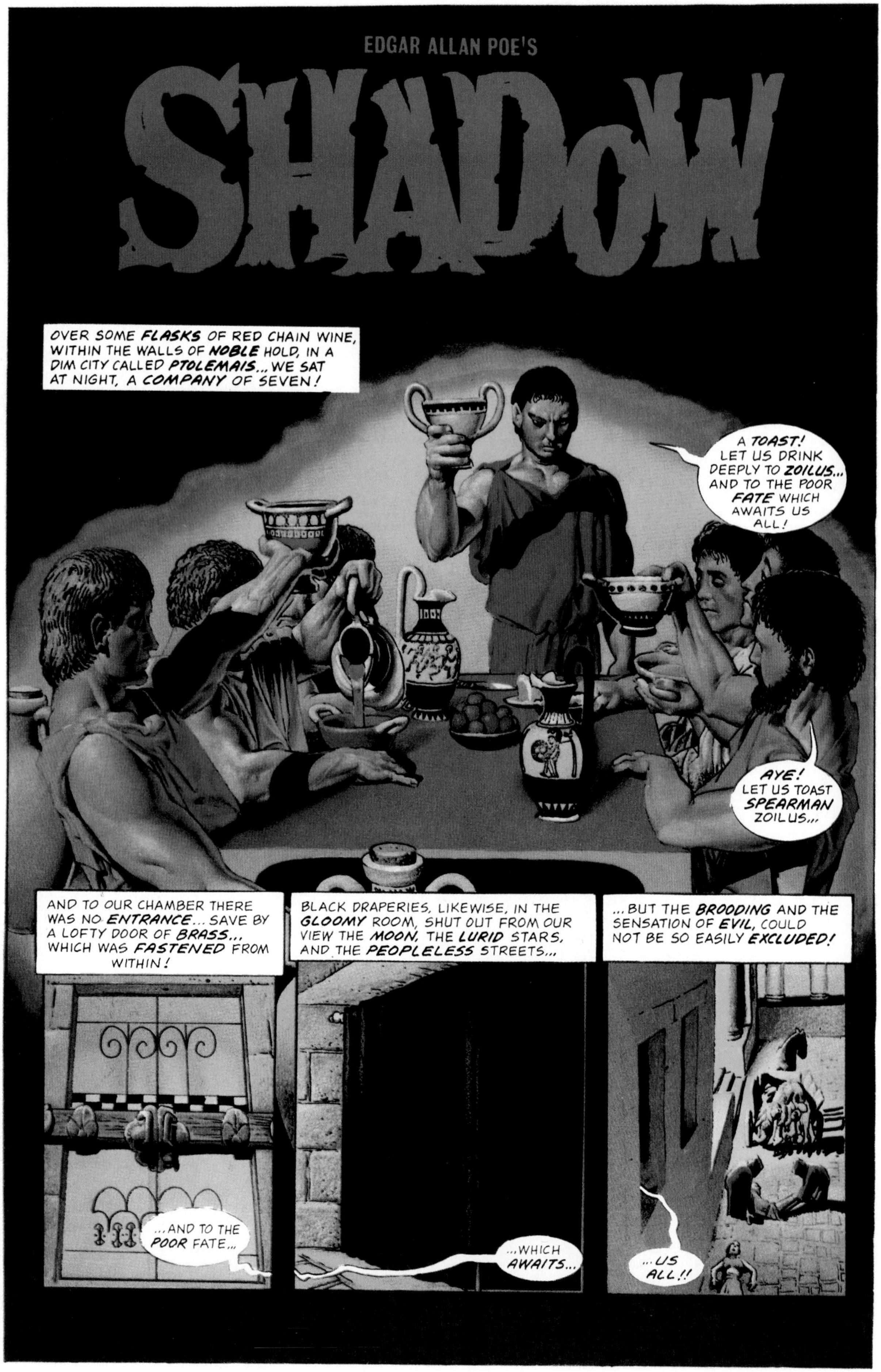
EDGAR ALLAN POE'S
SHADOW
OVER SOME FLASKS OF RED CHAIN WINE, WITHIN THE WALLS OF NOBLE HOLD, IN A DIM CITY CALLED PTOLEMAIS... WE SAT AT NIGHT, A COMPANY OF SEVEN!
A TOAST! LET US DRINK DEEPLY TO ZOILUS... AND TO THE POOR FATE WHICH AWAITS US ALL!
AYE! LET US TOAST SPEARMAN ZOILUS...
AND TO OUR CHAMBER THERE WAS NO ENTRANCE... SAVE BY A LOFTY DOOR OF BRASS... WHICH WAS FASTENED FROM WITHIN!
...AND TO THE POOR FATE...
BLACK DRAPERIES, LIKEWISE, IN THE GLOOMY ROOM, SHUT OUT FROM OUR VIEW THE MOON, THE LURID STARS, AND THE PEOPLELESS STREETS...
...WHICH AWAITS...
...BUT THE BROODING AND THE SENSATION OF EVIL, COULD NOT BE SO EASILY EXCLUDED!
...US ALL!!

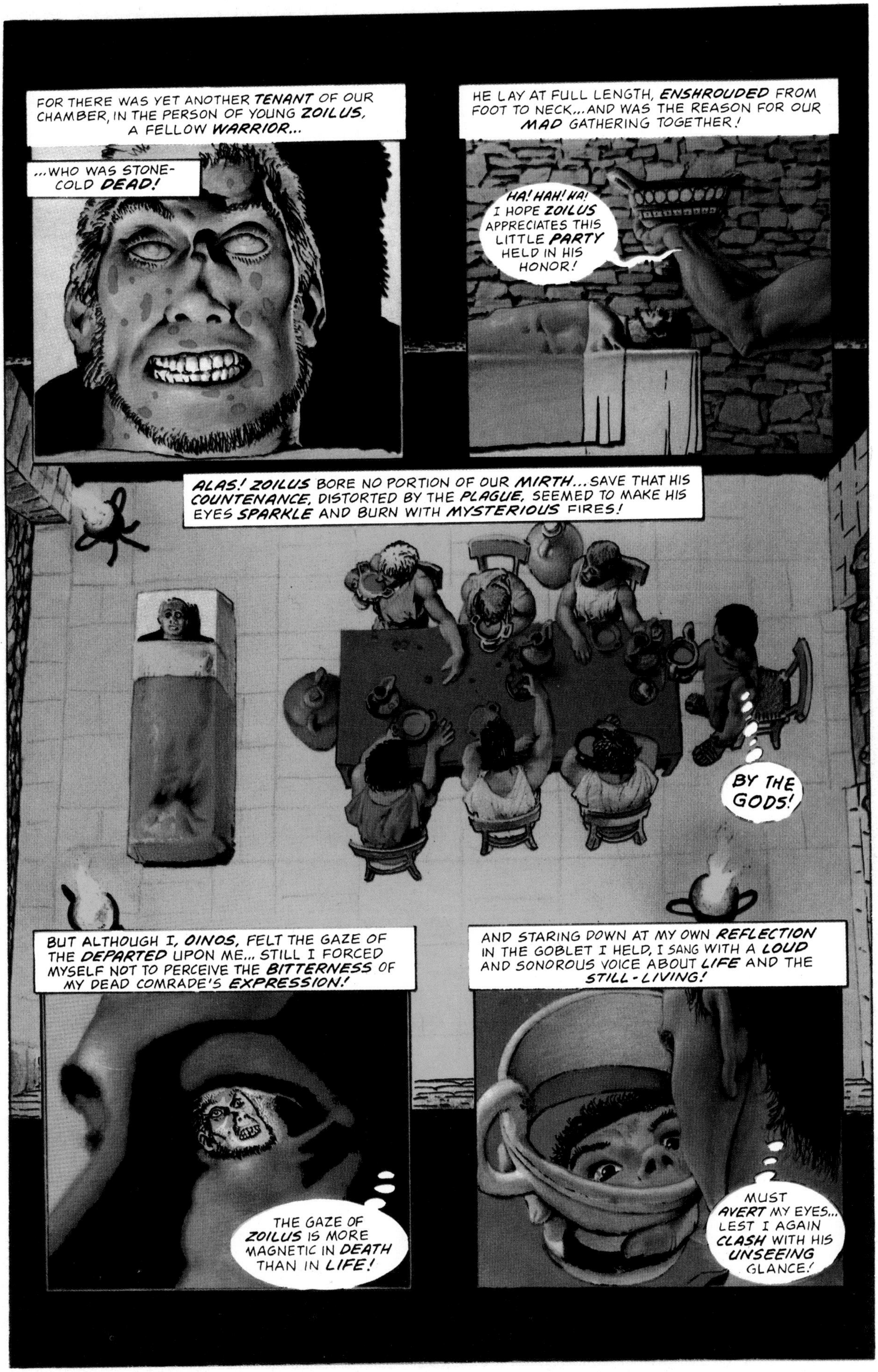

FOR THERE WAS YET ANOTHER TENANT OF OUR CHAMBER, IN THE PERSON OF YOUNG ZOILUS, A FELLOW WARRIOR...
...WHO WAS STONE-COLD DEAD!
HE LAY AT FULL LENGTH, ENSHROUDED FROM FOOT TO NECK...AND WAS THE REASON FOR OUR MAD GATHERING TOGETHER!
HA! HAH! HA! I HOPE ZOILUS APPRECIATES THIS LITTLE PARTY HELD IN HIS HONOR!
ALAS! ZOILUS BORE NO PORTION OF OUR MIRTH... SAVE THAT HIS COUNTENANCE, DISTORTED BY THE PLAGUE, SEEMED TO MAKE HIS EYES SPARKLE AND BURN WITH MYSTERIOUS FIRES!
BY THE GODS!
BUT ALTHOUGH I, OINOS, FELT THE GAZE OF THE DEPARTED UPON ME... STILL I FORCED MYSELF NOT TO PERCEIVE THE BITTERNESS OF MY DEAD COMRADE'S EXPRESSION!
THE GAZE OF ZOILUS IS MORE MAGNETIC IN DEATH THAN IN LIFE!
AND STARING DOWN AT MY OWN REFLECTION IN THE GOBLET I HELD, I SANG WITH A LOUD AND SONOROUS VOICE ABOUT LIFE AND THE STILL-LIVING!
MUST AVERT MY EYES... LEST I AGAIN CLASH WITH HIS UNSEEING GLANCE!

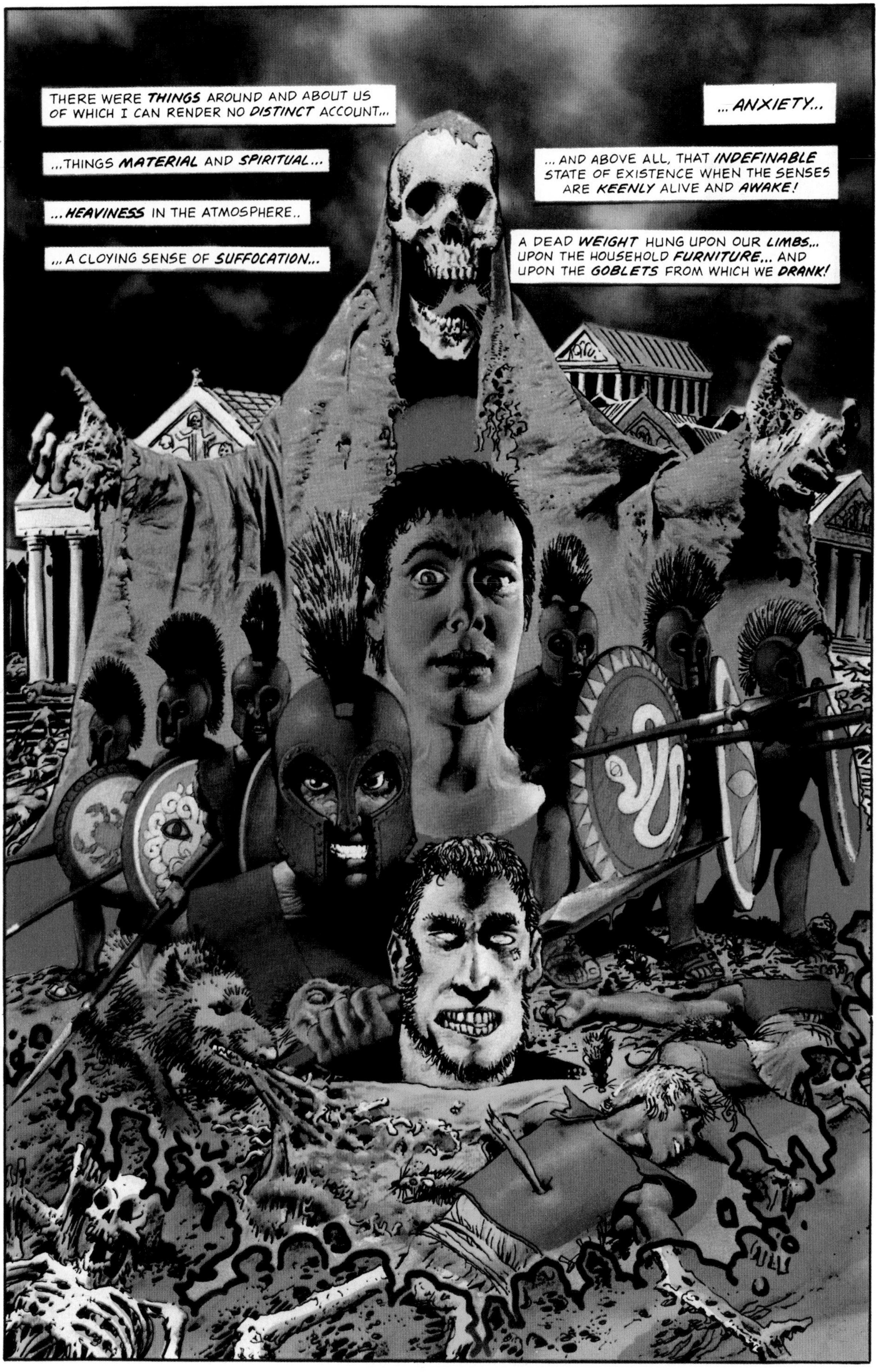
THERE WERE THINGS AROUND AND ABOUT US OF WHICH I CAN RENDER NO DISTINCT ACCOUNT...
...THINGS MATERIAL AND SPIRITUAL...
...HEAVINESS IN THE ATMOSPHERE..
...A CLOYING SENSE OF SUFFOCATION...
...ANXIETY...
...AND ABOVE ALL, THAT INDEFINABLE STATE OF EXISTENCE WHEN THE SENSES ARE KEENLY ALIVE AND AWAKE!
A DEAD WEIGHT HUNG UPON OUR LIMBS... UPON THE HOUSEHOLD FURNITURE... AND UPON THE GOBLETS FROM WHICH WE DRANK!

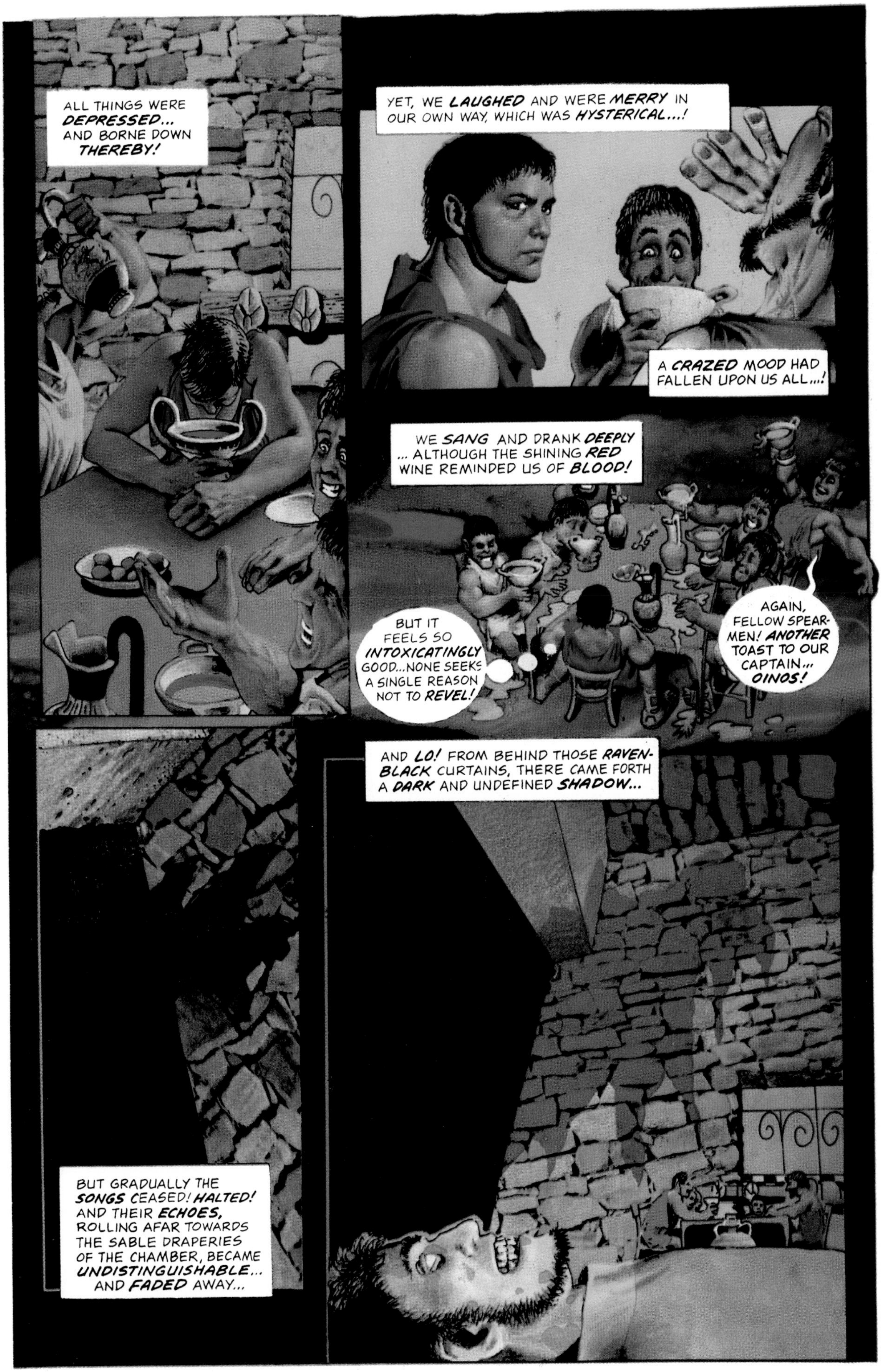
ALL THINGS WERE DEPRESSED... AND BORNE DOWN THEREBY!
YET, WE LAUGHED AND WERE MERRY IN OUR OWN WAY, WHICH WAS HYSTERICAL...!
A CRAZED MOOD HAD FALLEN UPON US ALL...!
WE SANG AND DRANK DEEPLY ... ALTHOUGH THE SHINING RED WINE REMINDED US OF BLOOD!
AGAIN, FELLOW SPEARMEN! ANOTHER TOAST TO OUR CAPTAIN... OINOS!
BUT IT FEELS SO INTOXICATINGLY GOOD...NONE SEEKS A SINGLE REASON NOT TO REVEL!
BUT GRADUALLY THE SONGS CEASED! HALTED! AND THEIR ECHOES, ROLLING AFAR TOWARDS THE SABLE DRAPERIES OF THE CHAMBER, BECAME UNDISTINGUISHABLE... AND FADED AWAY...
AND LO! FROM BEHIND THOSE RAVEN-BLACK CURTAINS, THERE CAME FORTH A DARK AND UNDEFINED SHADOW...

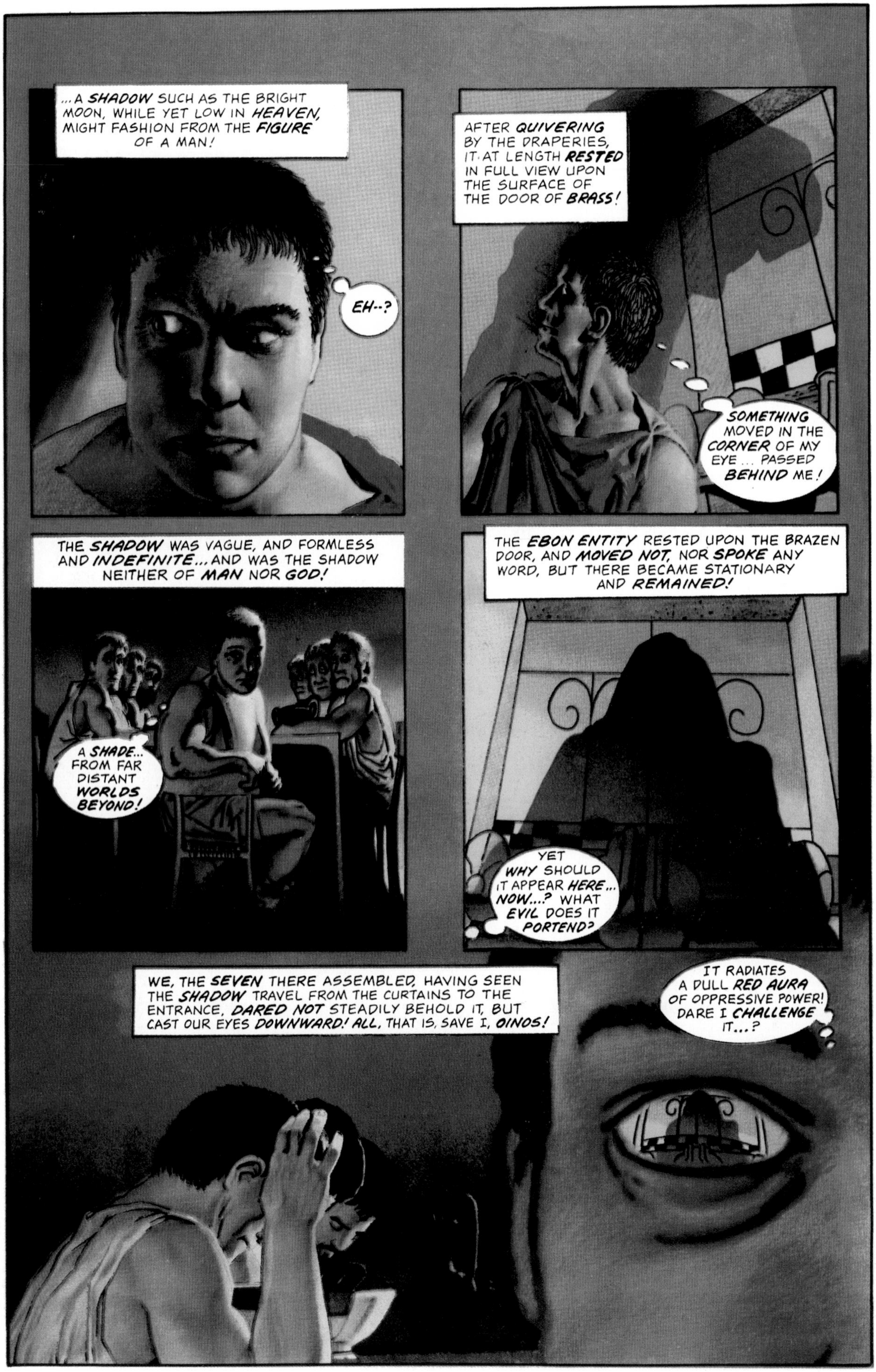
...A SHADOW SUCH AS THE BRIGHT MOON, WHILE YET LOW IN HEAVEN, MIGHT FASHION FROM THE FIGURE OF A MAN!
EH--?
AFTER QUIVERING BY THE DRAPERIES, IT AT LENGTH RESTED IN FULL VIEW UPON THE SURFACE OF THE DOOR OF BRASS!
SOMETHING MOVED IN THE CORNER OF MY EYE ... PASSED BEHIND ME!
THE SHADOW WAS VAGUE, AND FORMLESS AND INDEFINITE... AND WAS THE SHADOW NEITHER OF MAN NOR GOD!
A SHADE... FROM FAR DISTANT WORLDS BEYOND!
THE EBON ENTITY RESTED UPON THE BRAZEN DOOR, AND MOVED NOT, NOR SPOKE ANY WORD, BUT THERE BECAME STATIONARY AND REMAINED!
YET WHY SHOULD IT APPEAR HERE... NOW...? WHAT EVIL DOES IT PORTEND?
WE, THE SEVEN THERE ASSEMBLED, HAVING SEEN THE SHADOW TRAVEL FROM THE CURTAINS TO THE ENTRANCE, DARED NOT STEADILY BEHOLD IT, BUT CAST OUR EYES DOWNWARD! ALL, THAT IS, SAVE I, OINOS!
IT RADIATES A DULL RED AURA OF OPPRESSIVE POWER! DARE I CHALLENGE IT...?

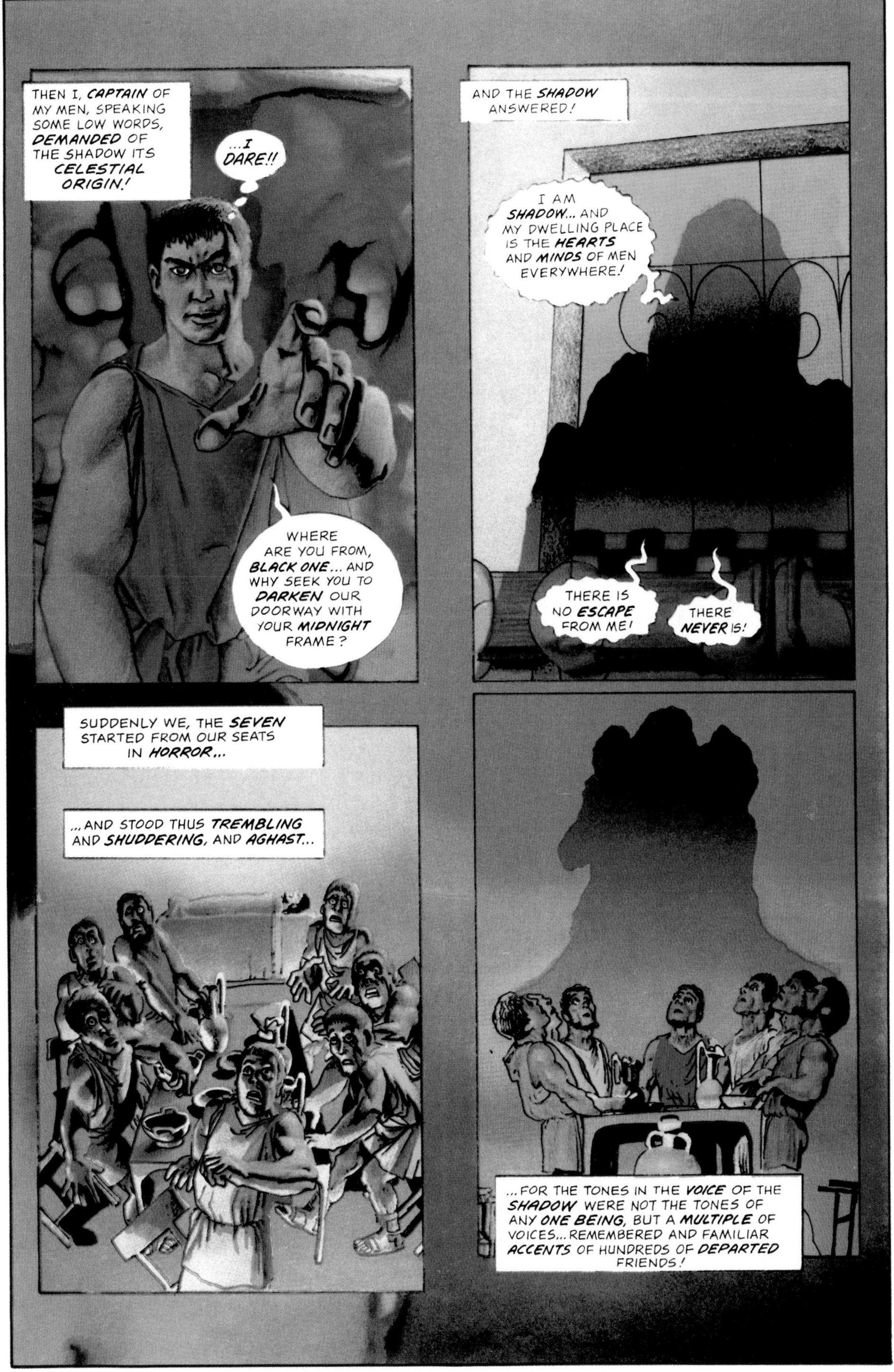

THEN I, CAPTAIN OF MY MEN, SPEAKING SOME LOW WORDS, DEMANDED OF THE SHADOW ITS CELESTIAL ORIGIN!
...I DARE!!
WHERE ARE YOU FROM, BLACK ONE... AND WHY SEEK YOU TO DARKEN OUR DOORWAY WITH YOUR MIDNIGHT FRAME?
AND THE SHADOW ANSWERED!
I AM SHADOW... AND MY DWELLING PLACE IS THE HEARTS AND MINDS OF MEN EVERYWHERE!
THERE IS NO ESCAPE FROM ME!
THERE NEVER IS!
SUDDENLY WE, THE SEVEN STARTED FROM OUR SEATS IN HORROR...
...AND STOOD THUS TREMBLING AND SHUDDERING, AND AGHAST...
...FOR THE TONES IN THE VOICE OF THE SHADOW WERE NOT THE TONES OF ANY ONE BEING, BUT A MULTIPLE OF VOICES... REMEMBERED AND FAMILIAR ACCENTS OF HUNDREDS OF DEPARTED FRIENDS!

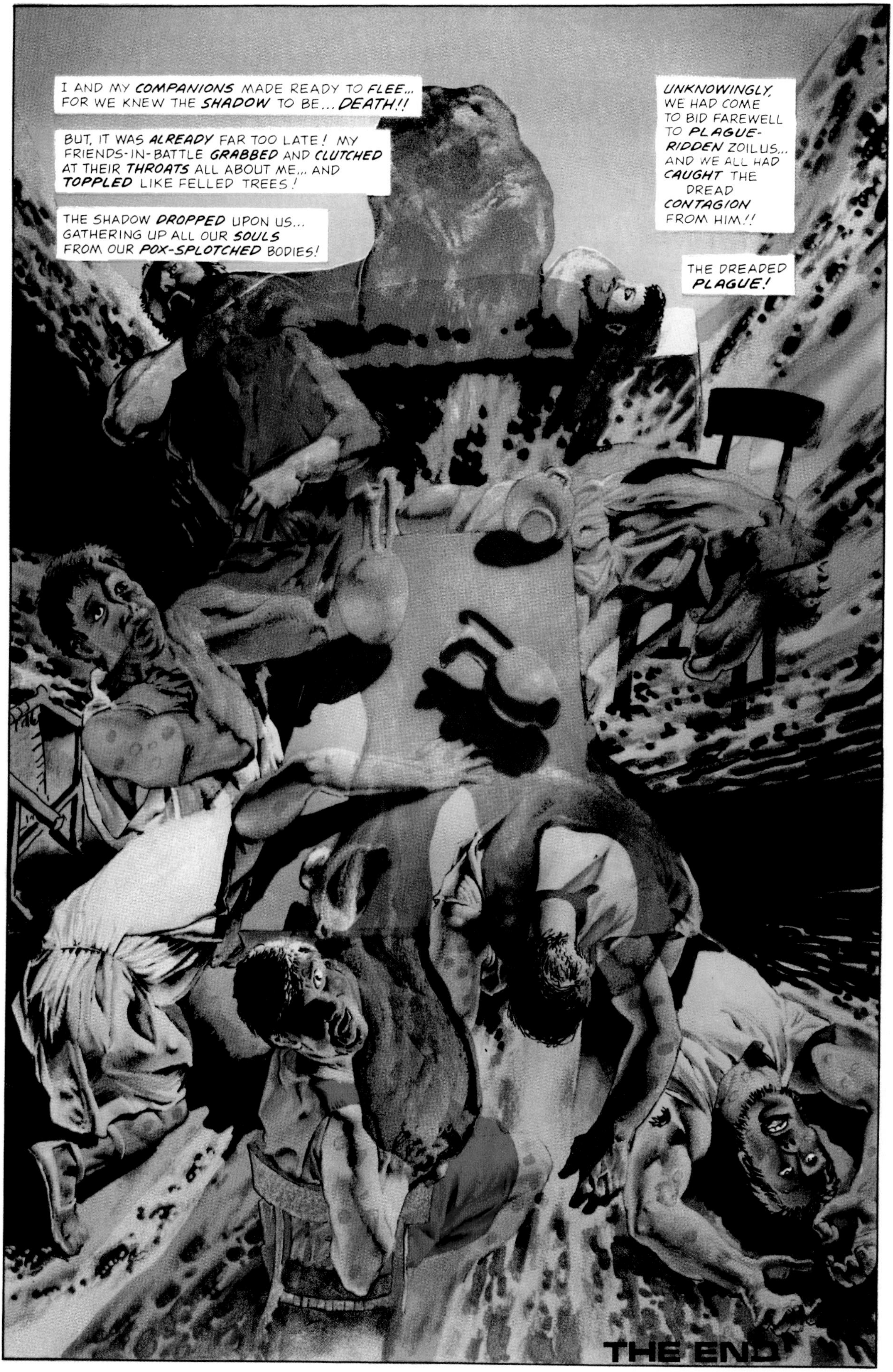
I AND MY COMPANIONS MADE READY TO FLEE... FOR WE KNEW THE SHADOW TO BE... DEATH!!
BUT, IT WAS ALREADY FAR TOO LATE! MY FRIENDS-IN-BATTLE GRABBED AND CLUTCHED AT THEIR THROATS ALL ABOUT ME... AND TOPPLED LIKE FELLED TREES!
THE SHADOW DROPPED UPON US... GATHERING UP ALL OUR SOULS FROM OUR POX-SPLOTCHED BODIES!
UNKNOWINGLY, WE HAD COME TO BID FAREWELL TO PLAGUE-RIDDEN ZOILUS... AND WE ALL HAD CAUGHT THE DREAD CONTAGION FROM HIM!!
THE DREADED PLAGUE!
THE END

PROLOGUE

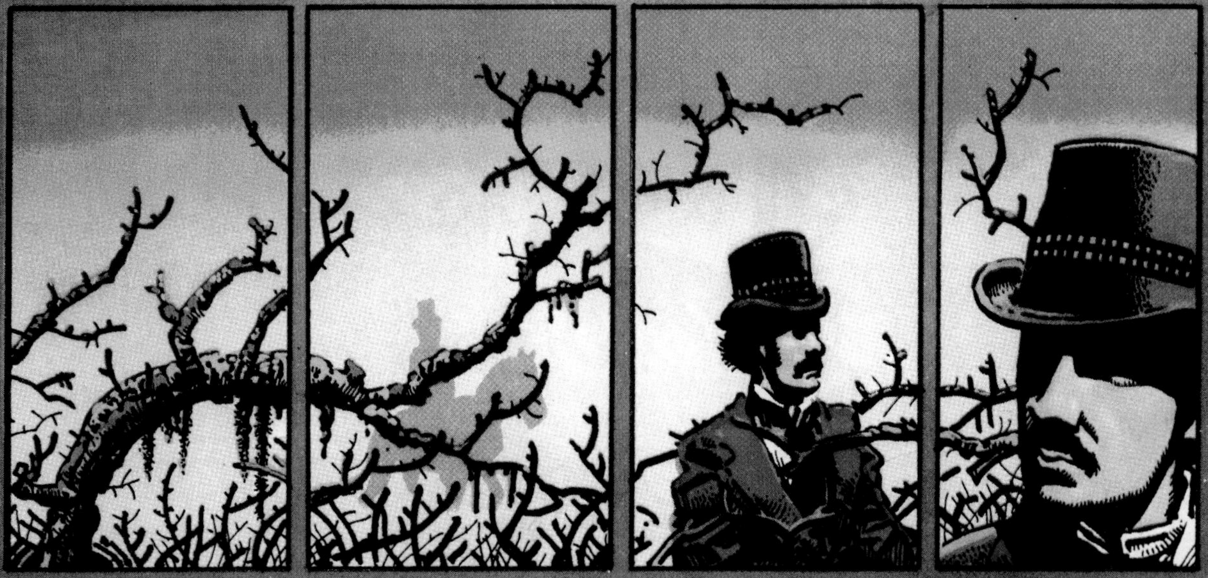

DURING THE WHOLE OF A DULL, DARK, AND SOUNDLESS DAY IN THE AUTUMN OF THE YEAR, WHEN THE CLOUDS WANDERED OPPRESSIVELY LOW AND WITH STRANGELY AGITATED MOVEMENT, I HAD BEEN PASSING ALONE ON HORSEBACK, THROUGH A SINGULARLY DREARY TRACT OF COUNTRY.

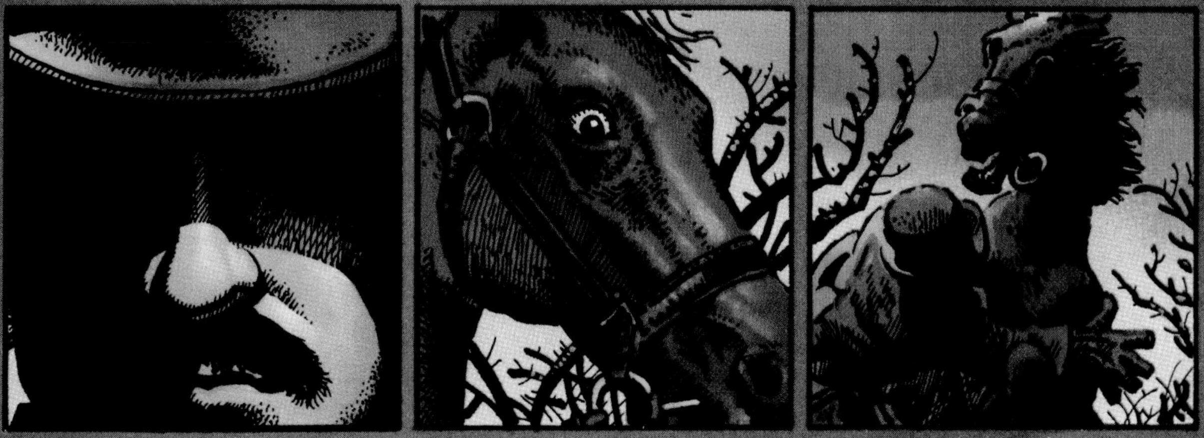

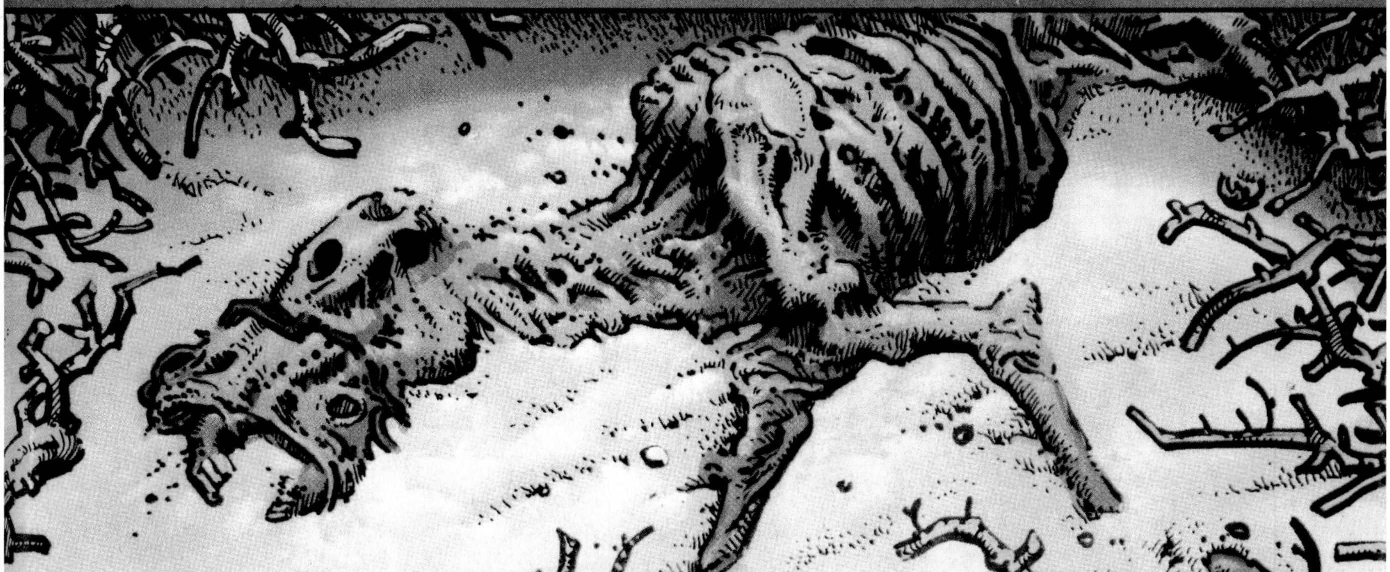

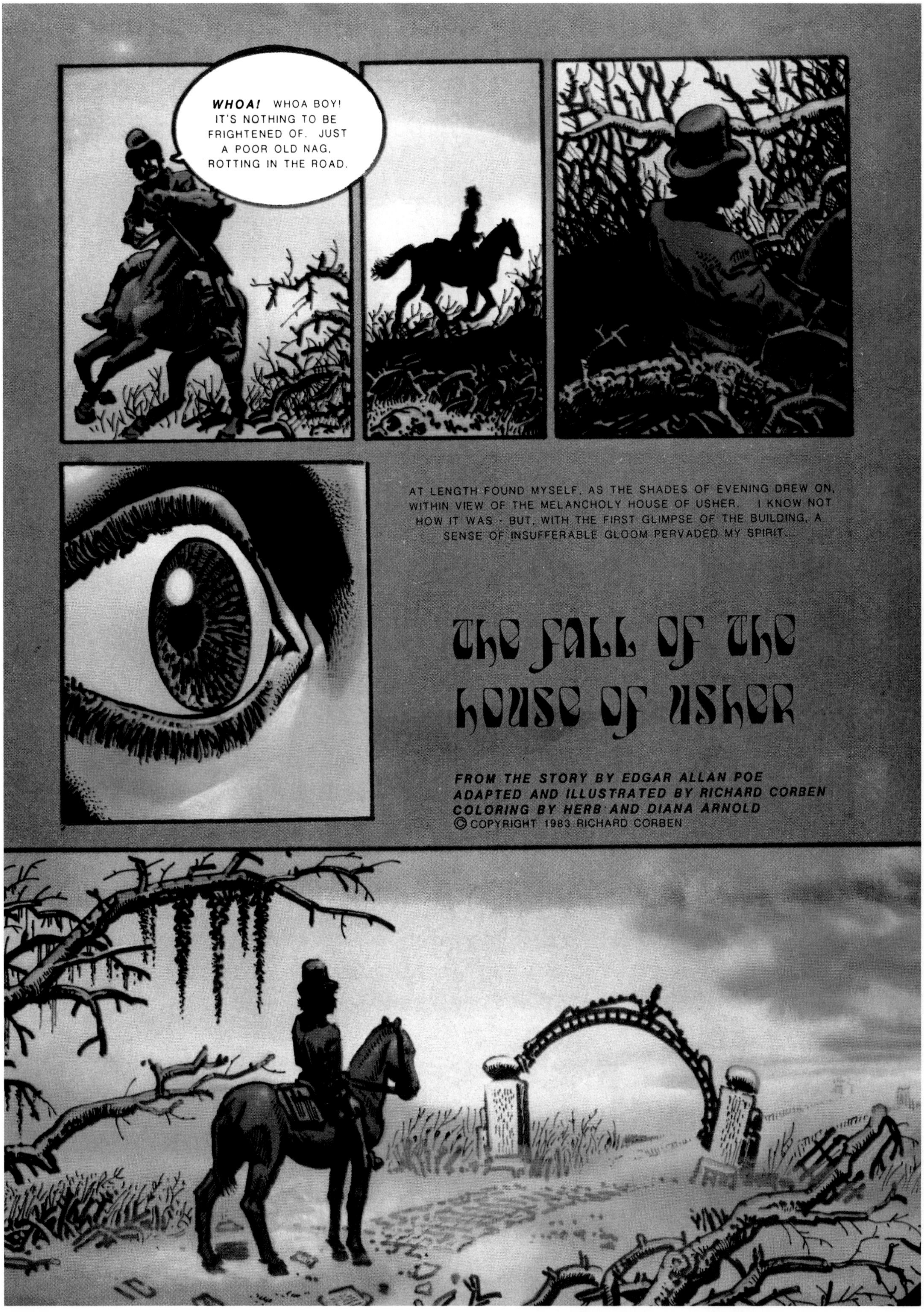
WHOA! WHOA BOY! IT'S NOTHING TO BE FRIGHTENED OF. JUST A POOR OLD NAG, ROTTING IN THE ROAD.
AT LENGTH FOUND MYSELF, AS THE SHADES OF EVENING DREW ON, WITHIN VIEW OF THE MELANCHOLY HOUSE OF USHER. I KNOW NOT HOW IT WAS - BUT, WITH THE FIRST GLIMPSE OF THE BUILDING, A SENSE OF INSUFFERABLE GLOOM PERVADED MY SPIRIT.
THE FALL OF THE HOUSE OF USHER
FROM THE STORY BY EDGAR ALLAN POE
ADAPTED AND ILLUSTRATED BY RICHARD CORBEN
COLORING BY HERB AND DIANA ARNOLD
© COPYRIGHT 1983 RICHARD CORBEN

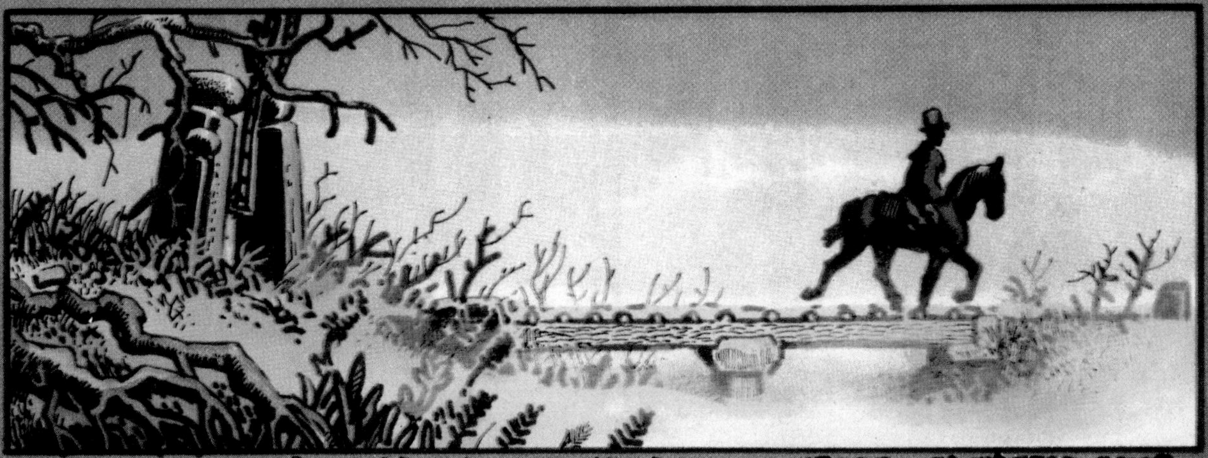
KLIP K-KLIP KLIP KLUMP K-KLUMP KLUMP K-KLUMP KLOP

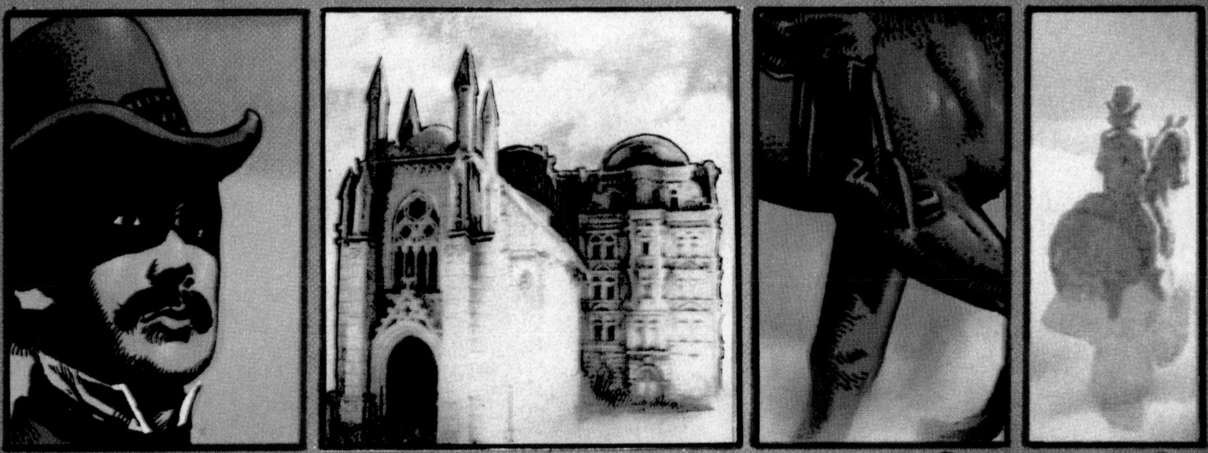
KLOP K-KLOP KLIP KLIP K-KLIP KLOP KLIP K-KLIP KLIP KLOP

THERE WAS AN ICINESS, A SINKING, A SICKENING OF THE HEART - AN UNREDEEMED DREARINESS OF THOUGHT, WHICH NO GOADING OF THE IMAGINATION COULD TORTURE INTO AUGHT OF THE SUBLIME. NEVERTHELESS, IN THIS MANSION OF UTTER DEPRESSION I NOW PROPOSED TO MYSELF A SOJOURN OF SOME WEEKS. RODERICK USHER HAD BEEN ONE OF MY BOON COMPANIONS IN BOYHOOD, BUT MANY YEARS HAD LAPSED SINCE OUR LAST MEETING.

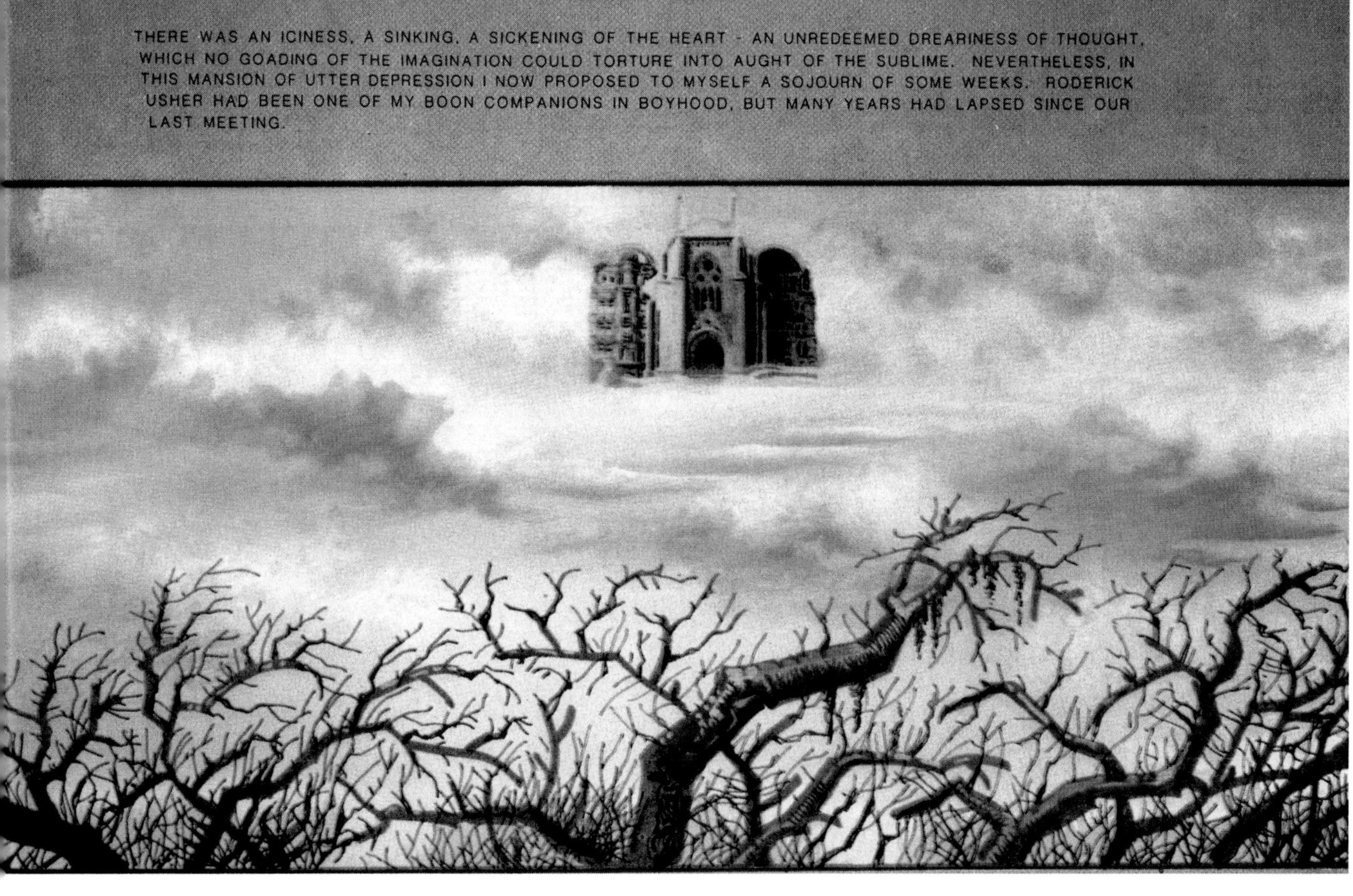

KLOP K-KLUP KLUP
KLIP K-KLIP KLOP
K-KLOP K-KLIP KLIP
KLOP K-KLOP KLIP

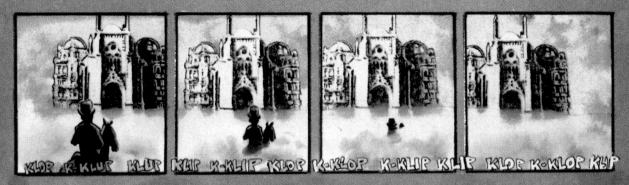

RODERICK'S LETTER HAD LATELY REACHED ME, BEGGING DESPERATELY FOR THIS VISIT. THE MANUSCRIPT GAVE EVIDENCE OF NERVOUS AGITATION. AND I ACCORDINGLY OBEYED FORTHWITH WHAT I STILL CONSIDERED A VERY SINGULAR SUMMONS.

WHA-? WHOA! ...AAAH!
KLOP K-KLOP KLUP K-KLIP
THUK SKRAK SKUFFLE SPLASH!
NO!
KER SPLASH!
BLURG BLURK
BUBBLE BUBBLE

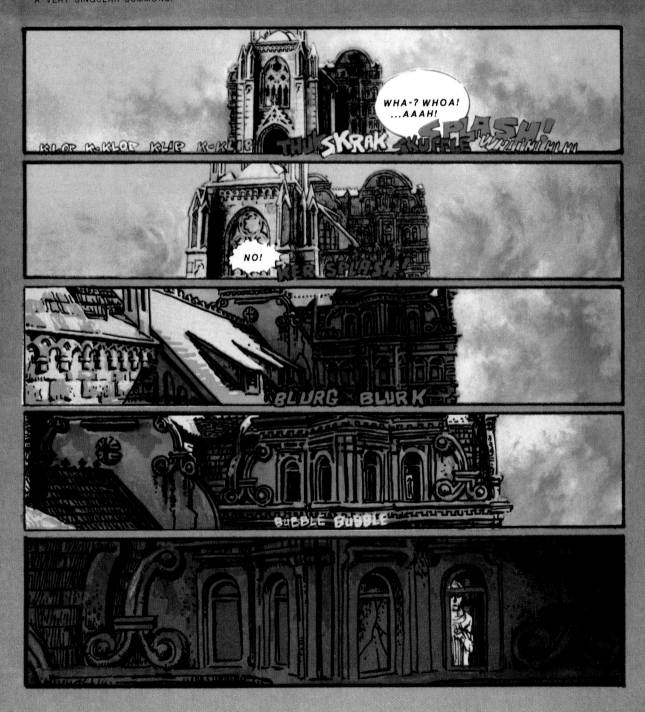

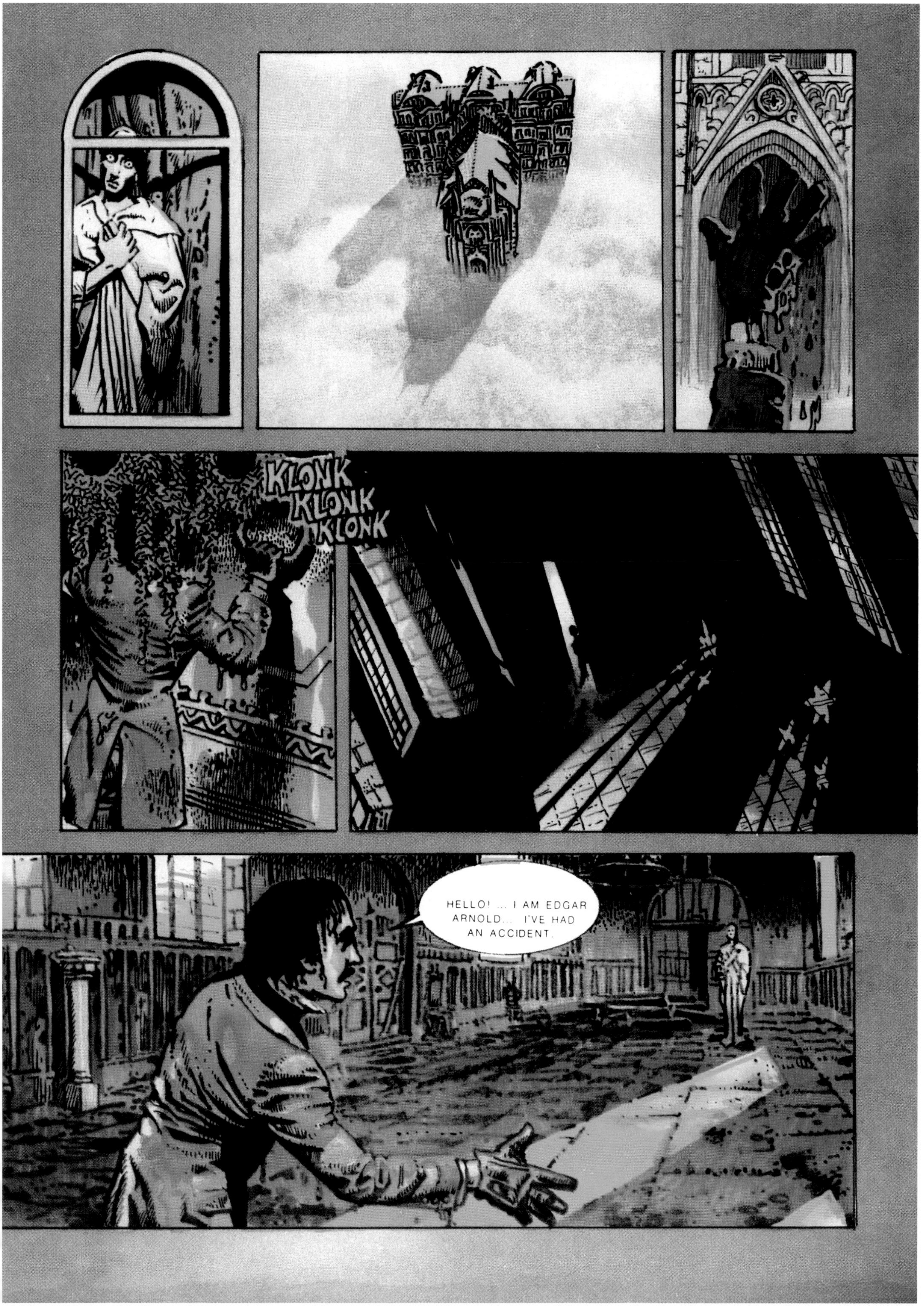
KLONK
KLONK
KLONK
HELLO! ... I AM EDGAR ARNOLD... I'VE HAD AN ACCIDENT.

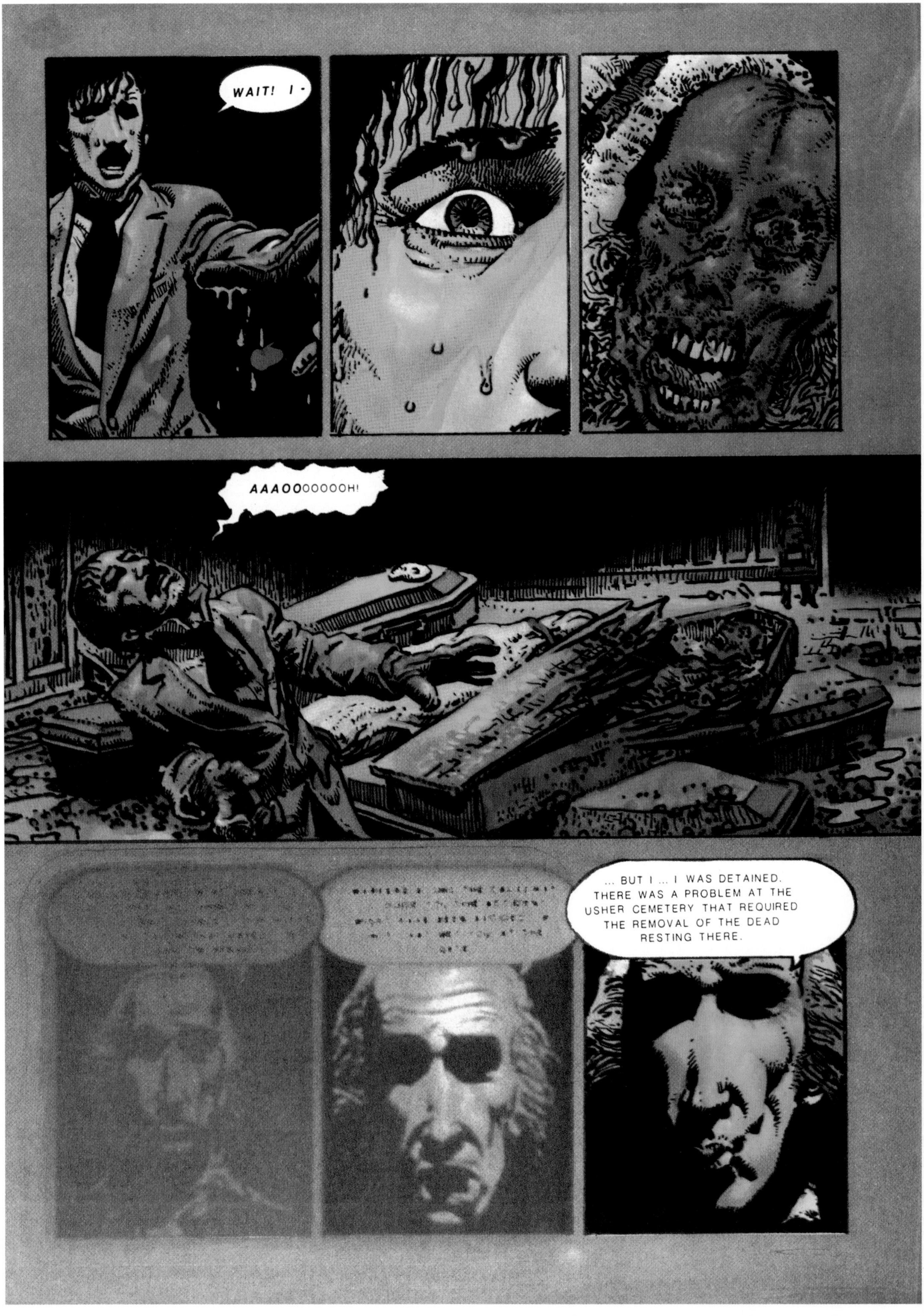

WAIT! I -
AAAOOOOOOOH!
... BUT I ... I WAS DETAINED. THERE WAS A PROBLEM AT THE USHER CEMETERY THAT REQUIRED THE REMOVAL OF THE DEAD RESTING THERE.

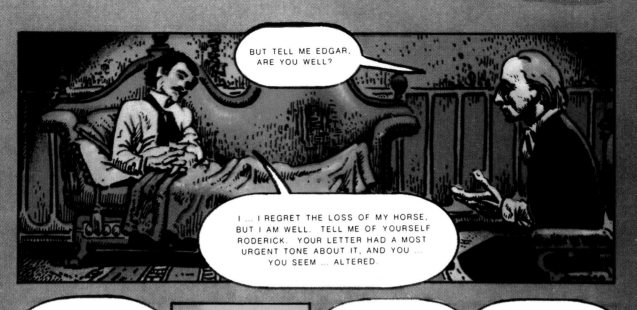

BUT TELL ME EDGAR, ARE YOU WELL?

I ... I REGRET THE LOSS OF MY HORSE, BUT I AM WELL. TELL ME OF YOURSELF RODERICK. YOUR LETTER HAD A MOST URGENT TONE ABOUT IT, AND YOU ... YOU SEEM ... ALTERED.

YES.. I HOPE YOU WILL REMAIN FOR AWHILE TO RELIEVE THE MORBID SOLITUDE THAT STEMS FROM MY MALADY.

IT IS A CONSTITUTIONAL AND FAMILY EVIL AND ONE FOR WHICH I DESPAIR TO FIND A REMEDY.

A NERVOUS AFFLICTION THAT DISPLAYS ITSELF IN A HOST OF UNNATURAL SENSATIONS ...

I SUFFER MUCH FROM AN EXTREME ACUTENESS OF THE SENSES ...

THE MOST INSIPID FOOD IS ALONE ENDURABLE: I CAN WEAR ONLY GARMENTS OF CERTAIN TEXTURE ...

THE ODORS OF ALL FLOWERS ARE OPPRESSIVE, MY EYES ARE TORTURED BY EVEN FAINT LIGHT, AND THERE ARE BUT A FEW PECULIAR SOUNDS THAT DO NOT INSPIRE ME WITH HORROR.

I DREAD THE EVENTS OF THE FUTURE, NOT IN THEMSELVES BUT IN THEIR INEVITABLE RESULTS. I HAVE, INDEED, NO ABHORRENCE OF DANGER, EXCEPT IN ITS ABSOLUTE EFFECT - IN *TERROR*. I FEEL THAT THE PERIOD WILL SOONER OR LATER ARRIVE WHEN I MUST ABANDON LIFE AND REASON TOGETHER IN SOME STRUGGLE WITH THE GRIM PHANTASM, *FEAR!*

... AND MY SISTER, THE LADY MADELINE, SUFFERS ALL AS I DO.

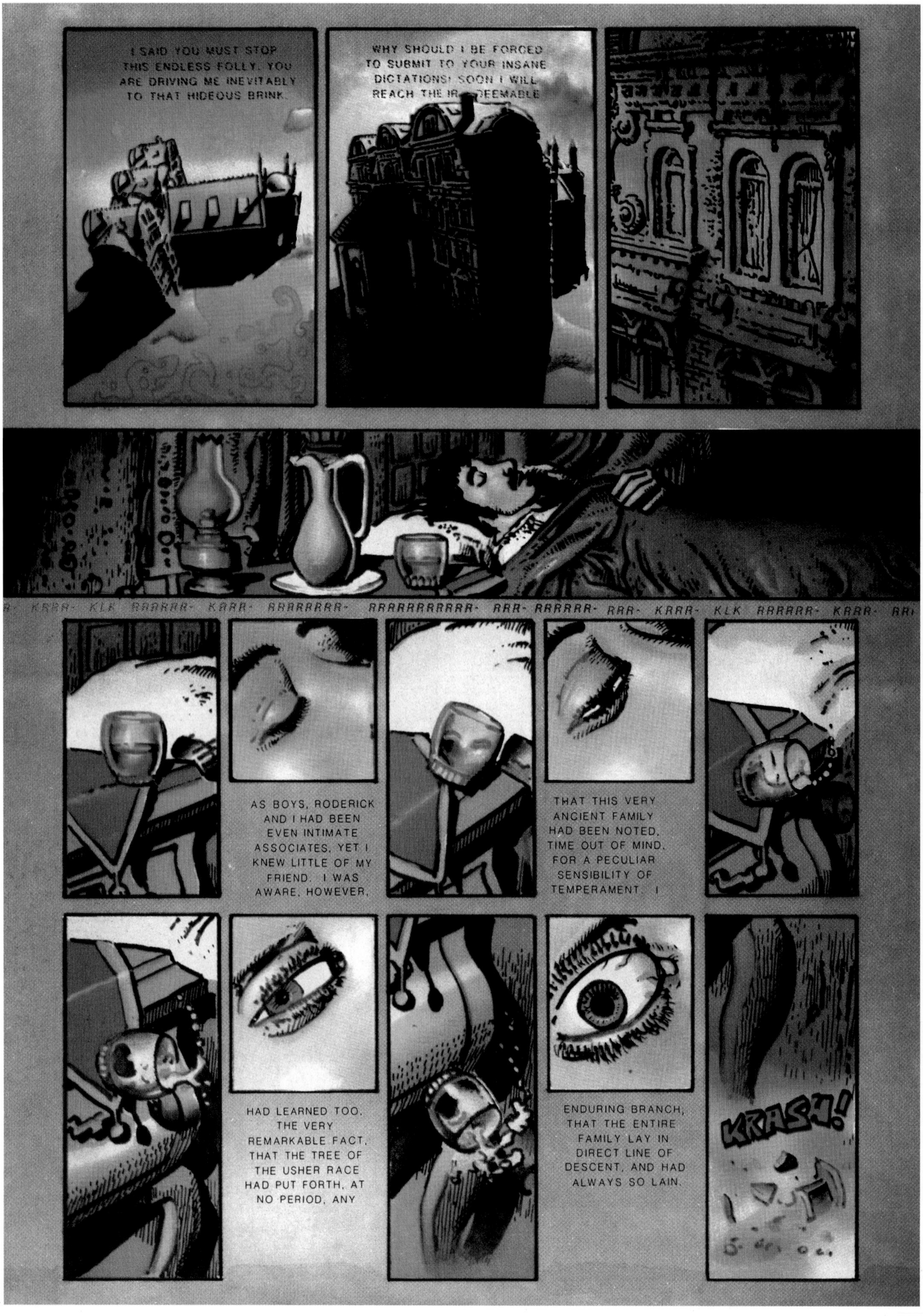
I SAID YOU MUST STOP THIS ENDLESS FOLLY. YOU ARE DRIVING ME INEVITABLY TO THAT HIDEOUS BRINK.
WHY SHOULD I BE FORCED TO SUBMIT TO YOUR INSANE DICTATIONS! SOON I WILL REACH THE IR DEEMABLE
KRRR- KLK RRRRRR- KRRR- RRRRRRRR- RRRRRRRRRRR- RRR- RRRRRR- RRR- KRRR- KLK RRRRRR- KRRR-
AS BOYS, RODERICK AND I HAD BEEN EVEN INTIMATE ASSOCIATES, YET I KNEW LITTLE OF MY FRIEND. I WAS AWARE, HOWEVER,
THAT THIS VERY ANCIENT FAMILY HAD BEEN NOTED, TIME OUT OF MIND, FOR A PECULIAR SENSIBILITY OF TEMPERAMENT. I
HAD LEARNED TOO, THE VERY REMARKABLE FACT, THAT THE TREE OF THE USHER RACE HAD PUT FORTH, AT NO PERIOD, ANY
ENDURING BRANCH, THAT THE ENTIRE FAMILY LAY IN DIRECT LINE OF DESCENT, AND HAD ALWAYS SO LAIN.
KRASH!

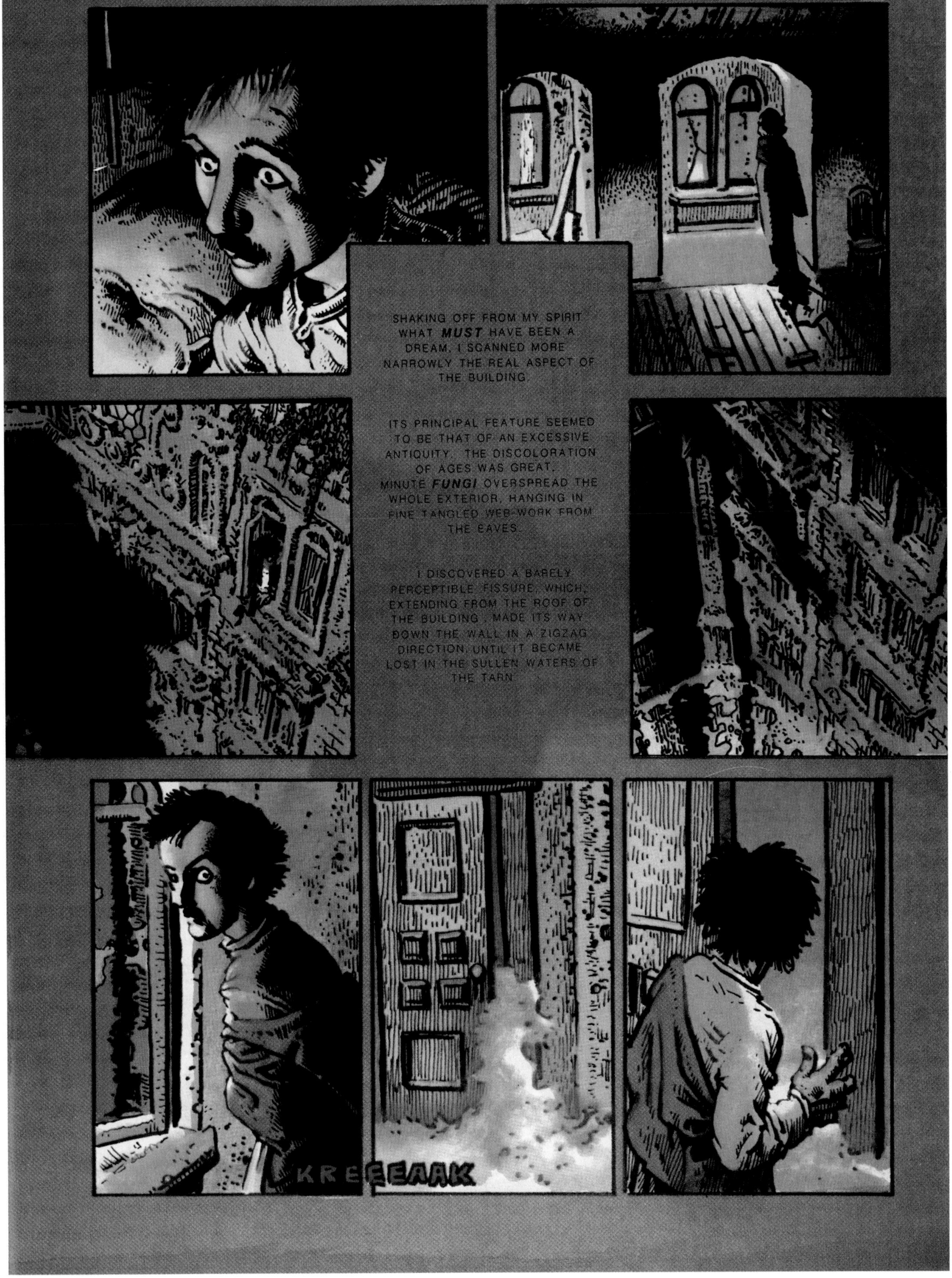
SHAKING OFF FROM MY SPIRIT WHAT MUST HAVE BEEN A DREAM, I SCANNED MORE NARROWLY THE REAL ASPECT OF THE BUILDING.
ITS PRINCIPAL FEATURE SEEMED TO BE THAT OF AN EXCESSIVE ANTIQUITY. THE DISCOLORATION OF AGES WAS GREAT. MINUTE FUNGI OVERSPREAD THE WHOLE EXTERIOR, HANGING IN FINE TANGLED WEB-WORK FROM THE EAVES.
I DISCOVERED A BARELY PERCEPTIBLE FISSURE, WHICH, EXTENDING FROM THE ROOF OF THE BUILDING, MADE ITS WAY DOWN THE WALL IN A ZIGZAG DIRECTION, UNTIL IT BECAME LOST IN THE SULLEN WATERS OF THE TARN.
KREEEAAK

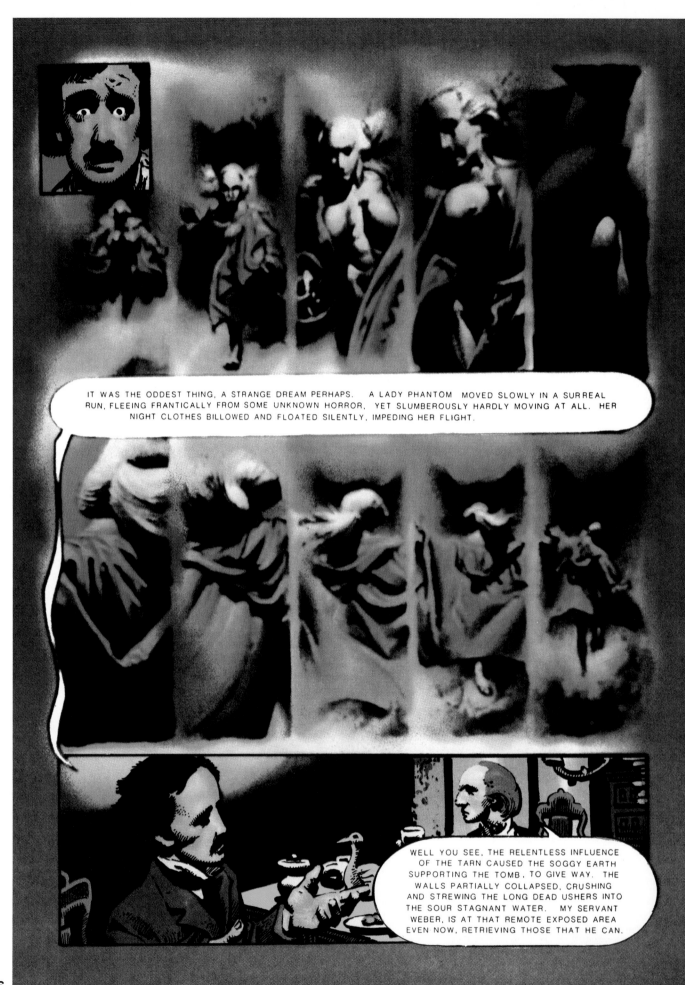

IT WAS THE ODDEST THING, A STRANGE DREAM PERHAPS. A LADY PHANTOM MOVED SLOWLY IN A SURREAL RUN, FLEEING FRANTICALLY FROM SOME UNKNOWN HORROR, YET SLUMBEROUSLY HARDLY MOVING AT ALL. HER NIGHT CLOTHES BILLOWED AND FLOATED SILENTLY, IMPEDING HER FLIGHT.

WELL YOU SEE, THE RELENTLESS INFLUENCE OF THE TARN CAUSED THE SOGGY EARTH SUPPORTING THE TOMB, TO GIVE WAY. THE WALLS PARTIALLY COLLAPSED, CRUSHING AND STREWING THE LONG DEAD USHERS INTO THE SOUR STAGNANT WATER. MY SERVANT WEBER, IS AT THAT REMOTE EXPOSED AREA EVEN NOW, RETRIEVING THOSE THAT HE CAN.

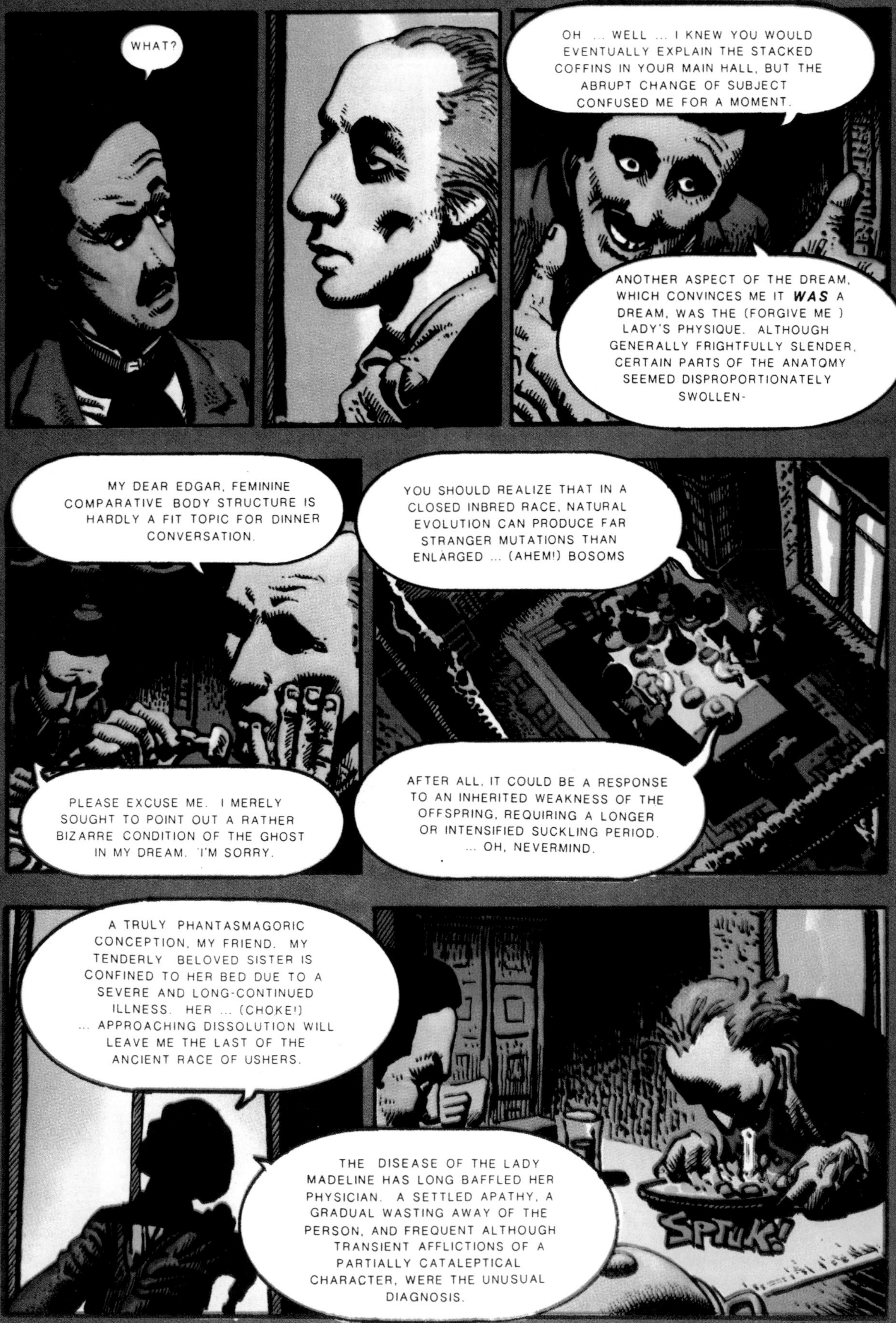
WHAT?
OH ... WELL ... I KNEW YOU WOULD EVENTUALLY EXPLAIN THE STACKED COFFINS IN YOUR MAIN HALL, BUT THE ABRUPT CHANGE OF SUBJECT CONFUSED ME FOR A MOMENT.
ANOTHER ASPECT OF THE DREAM, WHICH CONVINCES ME IT WAS A DREAM, WAS THE (FORGIVE ME) LADY'S PHYSIQUE. ALTHOUGH GENERALLY FRIGHTFULLY SLENDER, CERTAIN PARTS OF THE ANATOMY SEEMED DISPROPORTIONATELY SWOLLEN-
MY DEAR EDGAR, FEMININE COMPARATIVE BODY STRUCTURE IS HARDLY A FIT TOPIC FOR DINNER CONVERSATION.
PLEASE EXCUSE ME. I MERELY SOUGHT TO POINT OUT A RATHER BIZARRE CONDITION OF THE GHOST IN MY DREAM. I'M SORRY.
YOU SHOULD REALIZE THAT IN A CLOSED INBRED RACE, NATURAL EVOLUTION CAN PRODUCE FAR STRANGER MUTATIONS THAN ENLARGED ... (AHEM!) BOSOMS
AFTER ALL, IT COULD BE A RESPONSE TO AN INHERITED WEAKNESS OF THE OFFSPRING, REQUIRING A LONGER OR INTENSIFIED SUCKLING PERIOD. ... OH, NEVERMIND.
A TRULY PHANTASMAGORIC CONCEPTION, MY FRIEND. MY TENDERLY BELOVED SISTER IS CONFINED TO HER BED DUE TO A SEVERE AND LONG-CONTINUED ILLNESS. HER ... (CHOKE!) ... APPROACHING DISSOLUTION WILL LEAVE ME THE LAST OF THE ANCIENT RACE OF USHERS.
THE DISEASE OF THE LADY MADELINE HAS LONG BAFFLED HER PHYSICIAN. A SETTLED APATHY, A GRADUAL WASTING AWAY OF THE PERSON, AND FREQUENT ALTHOUGH TRANSIENT AFFLICTIONS OF A PARTIALLY CATALEPTICAL CHARACTER, WERE THE UNUSUAL DIAGNOSIS.
SPTUK!

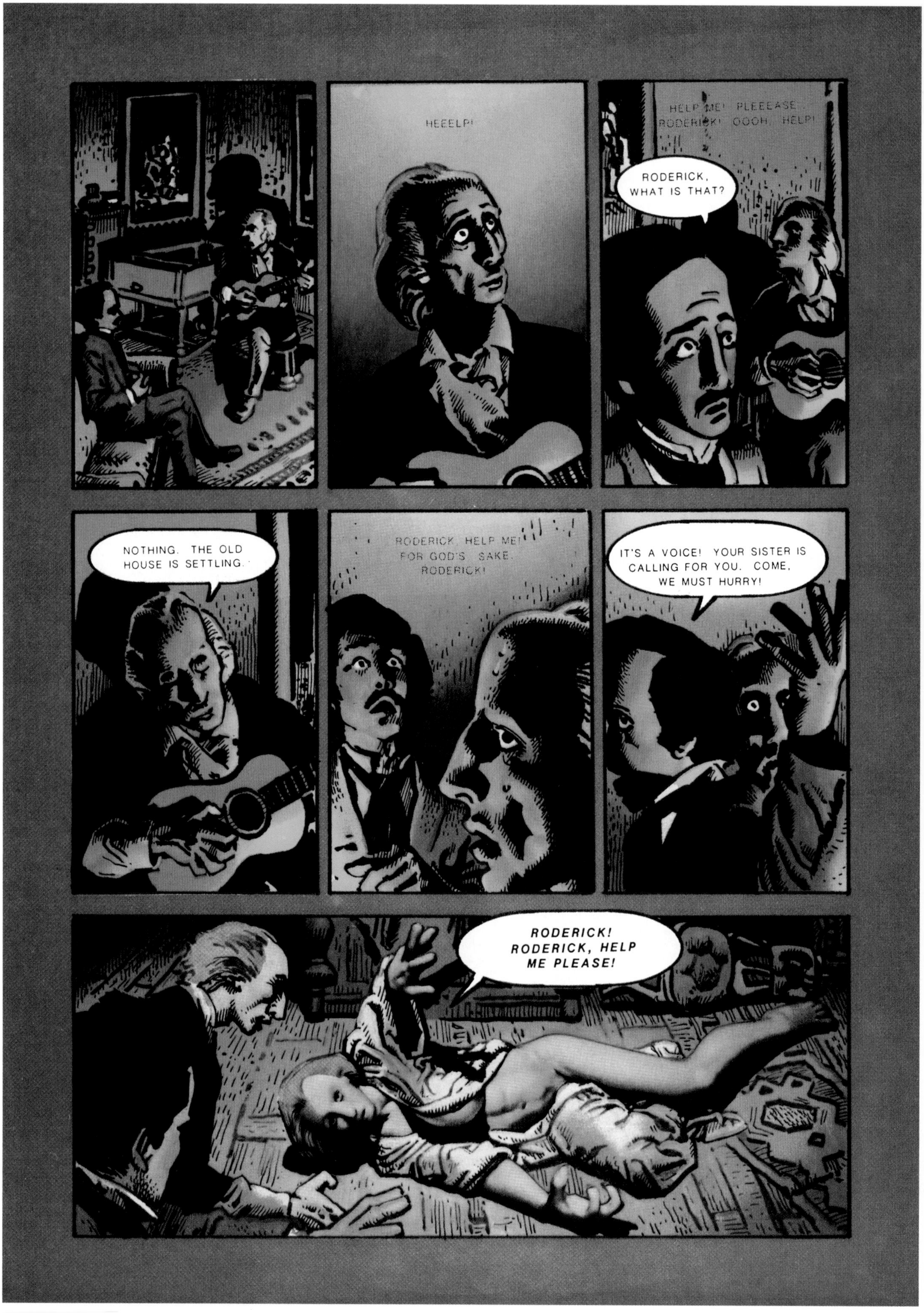
HEEELP!
HELP ME! PLEEEASE. RODERICK! OOOH, HELP!
RODERICK, WHAT IS THAT?
NOTHING. THE OLD HOUSE IS SETTLING.
RODERICK, HELP ME! FOR GOD'S SAKE. RODERICK!
IT'S A VOICE! YOUR SISTER IS CALLING FOR YOU. COME, WE MUST HURRY!
RODERICK! RODERICK, HELP ME PLEASE!

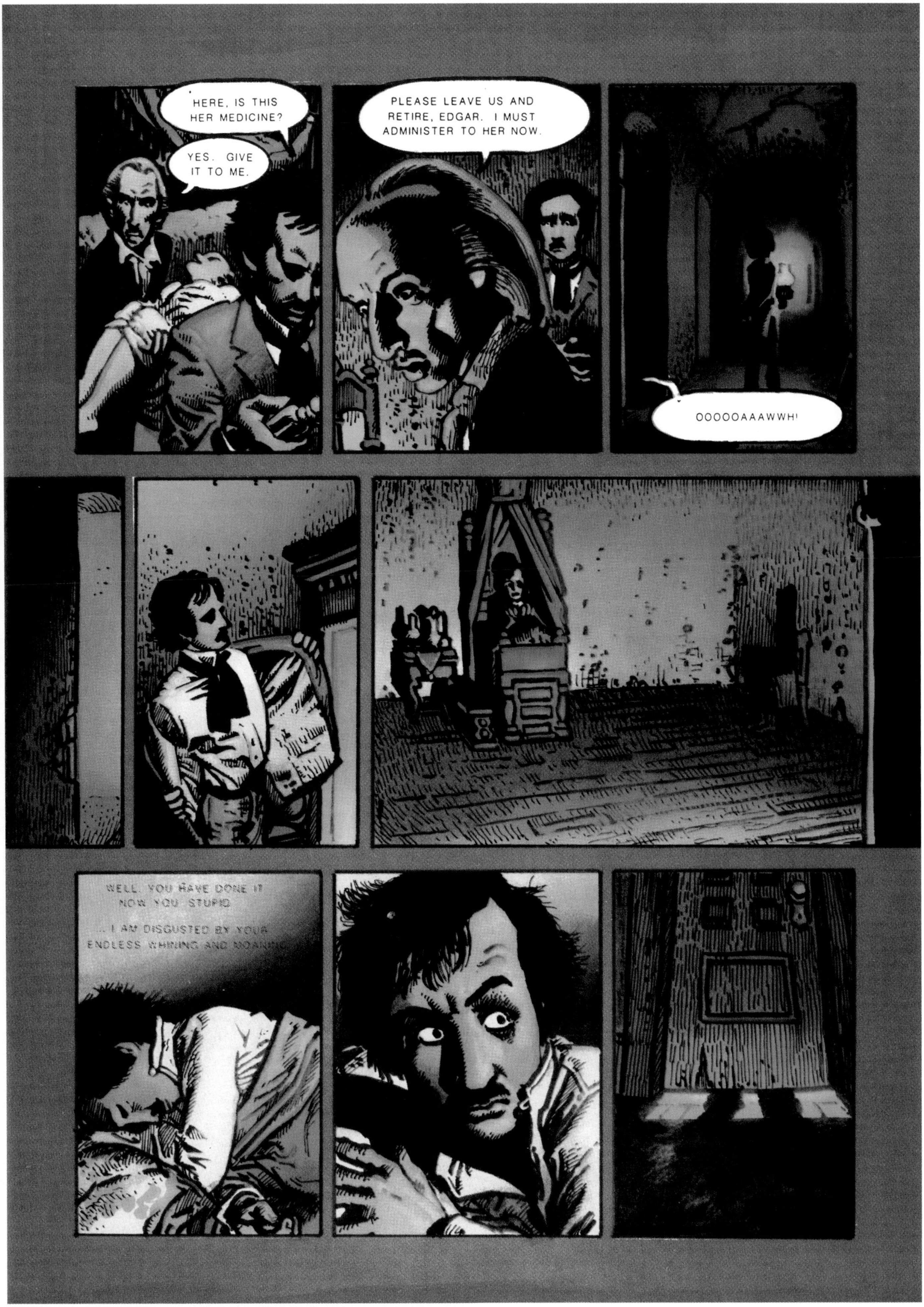
HERE, IS THIS HER MEDICINE?
YES. GIVE IT TO ME.
PLEASE LEAVE US AND RETIRE, EDGAR. I MUST ADMINISTER TO HER NOW.
OOOOOAAAWWH!
WELL. YOU HAVE DONE IT NOW YOU STUPID
... I AM DISGUSTED BY YOUR ENDLESS WHINING AND MOANING

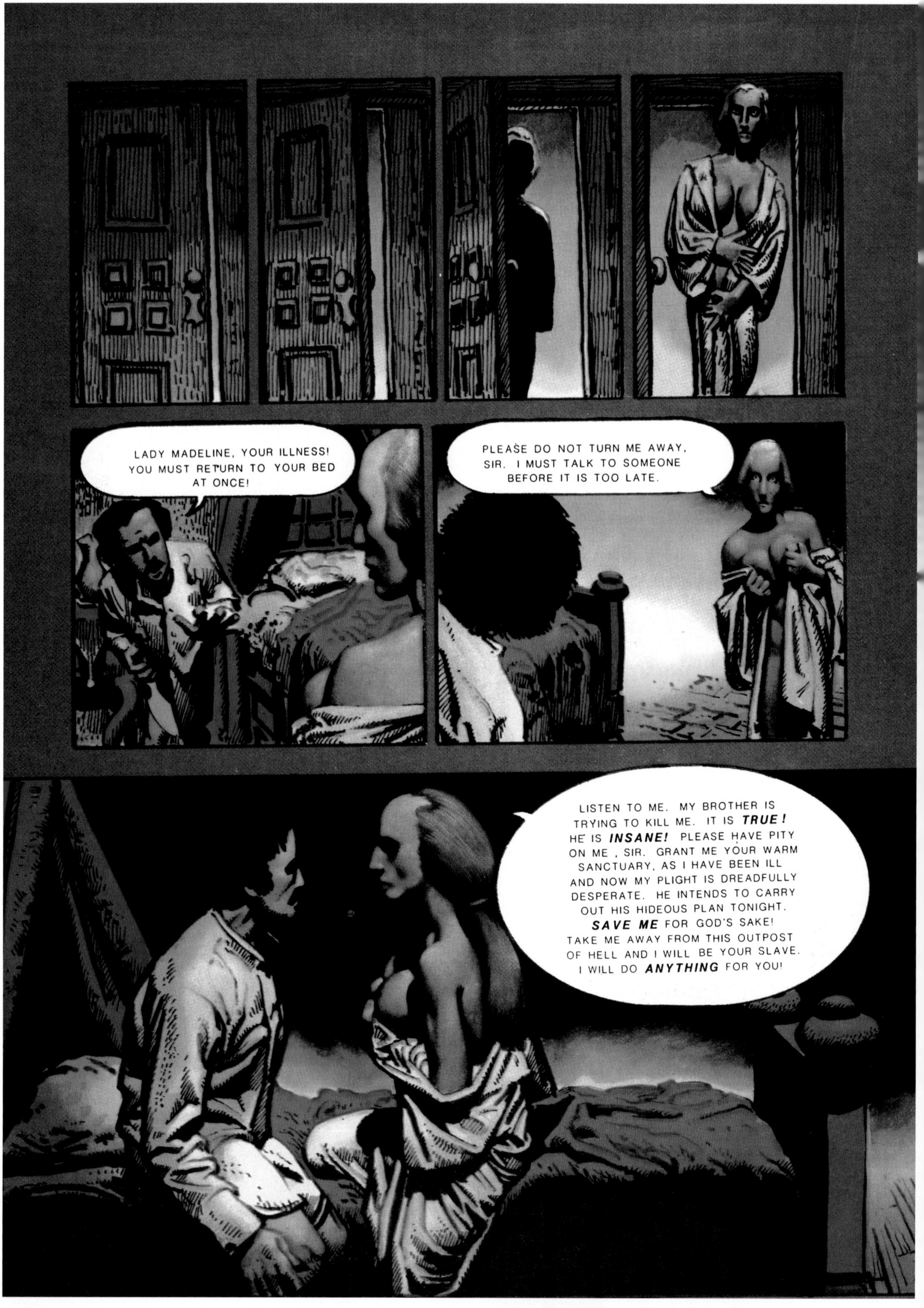
LADY MADELINE, YOUR ILLNESS! YOU MUST RETURN TO YOUR BED AT ONCE!
PLEASE DO NOT TURN ME AWAY, SIR. I MUST TALK TO SOMEONE BEFORE IT IS TOO LATE.
LISTEN TO ME. MY BROTHER IS TRYING TO KILL ME. IT IS **TRUE!** HE IS **INSANE!** PLEASE HAVE PITY ON ME, SIR. GRANT ME YOUR WARM SANCTUARY, AS I HAVE BEEN ILL AND NOW MY PLIGHT IS DREADFULLY DESPERATE. HE INTENDS TO CARRY OUT HIS HIDEOUS PLAN TONIGHT. **SAVE ME** FOR GOD'S SAKE! TAKE ME AWAY FROM THIS OUTPOST OF HELL AND I WILL BE YOUR SLAVE. I WILL DO **ANYTHING** FOR YOU!

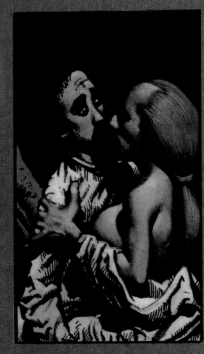

WANDERERS IN THAT HAPPY VALLEY
THROUGH TWO LUMINOUS WINDOWS SAW
SPIRITS MOVING MUSICALLY
TO A LUTE'S WELL-TUNED LAW,
ROUND ABOUT A THRONE, WHERE SITTING,
(PORPHYROGENE!)
IN STATE HIS GLORY WELL BEFITTING,
THE RULER OF THE REALM WAS SEEN.

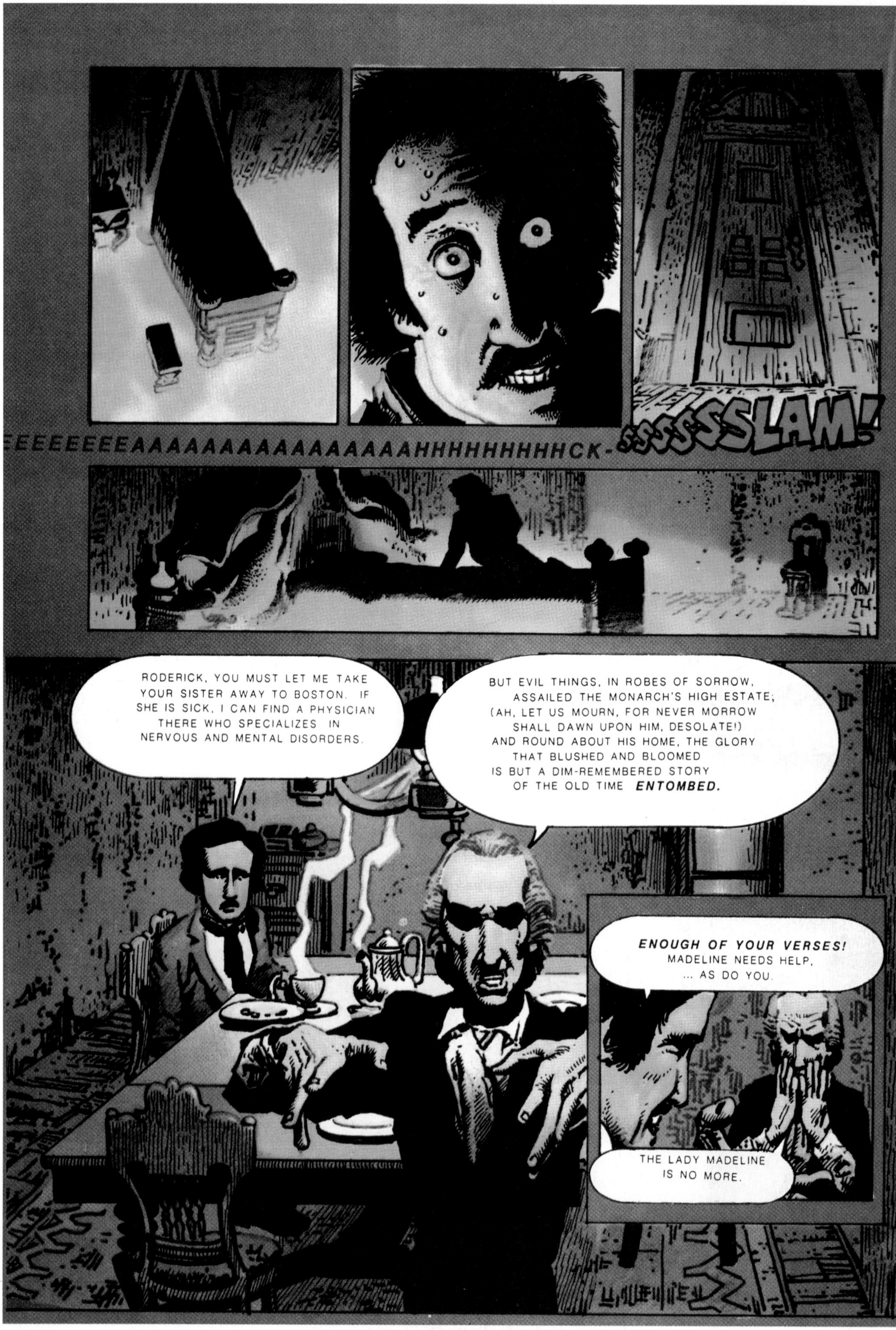
EEEEEEEEEAAAAAAAAAAAAAAAAAHHHHHHHHHCK-
SSSSSLAM!
RODERICK, YOU MUST LET ME TAKE YOUR SISTER AWAY TO BOSTON. IF SHE IS SICK, I CAN FIND A PHYSICIAN THERE WHO SPECIALIZES IN NERVOUS AND MENTAL DISORDERS.
BUT EVIL THINGS, IN ROBES OF SORROW, ASSAILED THE MONARCH'S HIGH ESTATE; (AH, LET US MOURN, FOR NEVER MORROW SHALL DAWN UPON HIM, DESOLATE!) AND ROUND ABOUT HIS HOME, THE GLORY THAT BLUSHED AND BLOOMED IS BUT A DIM-REMEMBERED STORY OF THE OLD TIME ENTOMBED.
ENOUGH OF YOUR VERSES! MADELINE NEEDS HELP, ... AS DO YOU.
THE LADY MADELINE IS NO MORE.

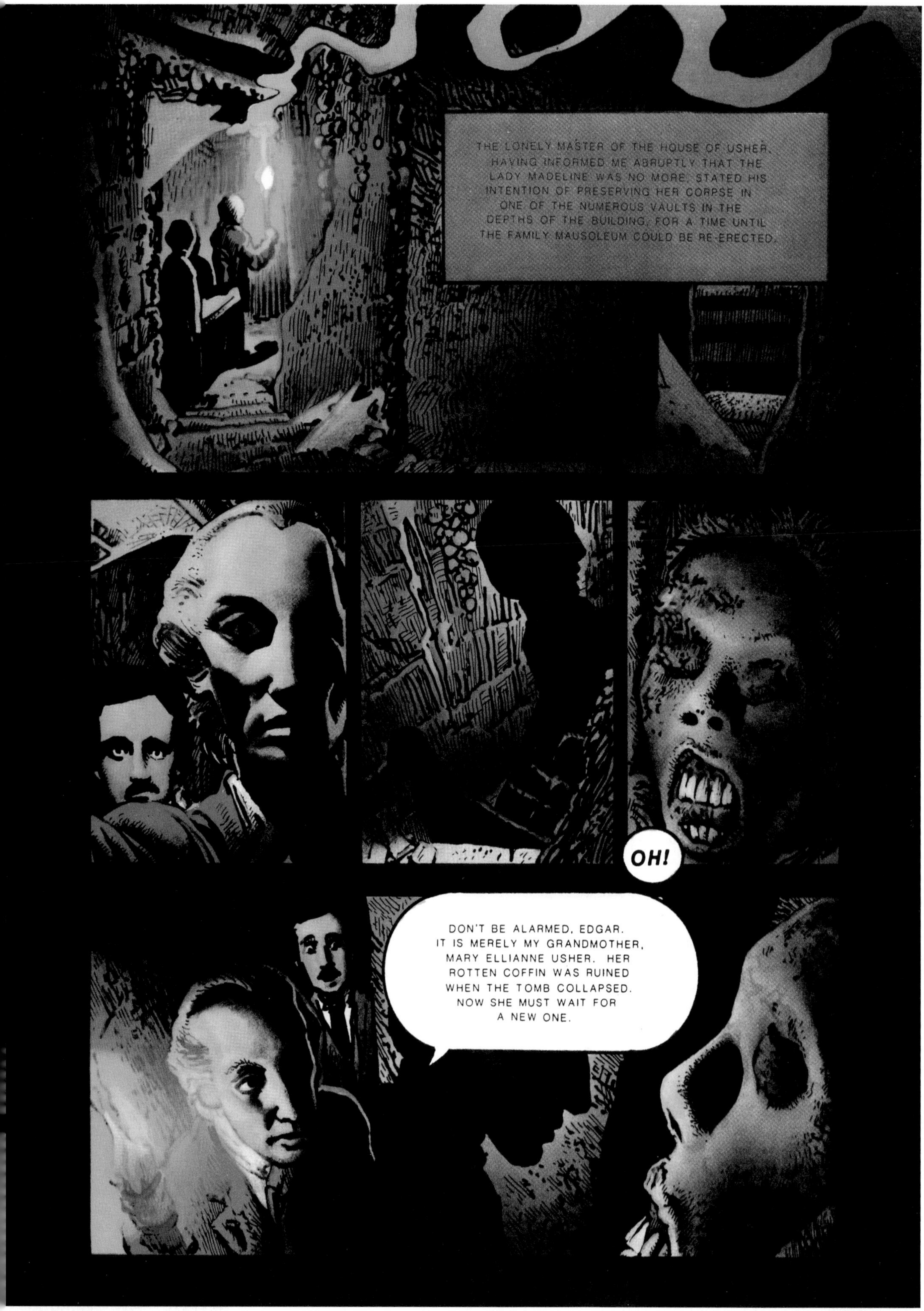
THE LONELY MASTER OF THE HOUSE OF USHER, HAVING INFORMED ME ABRUPTLY THAT THE LADY MADELINE WAS NO MORE, STATED HIS INTENTION OF PRESERVING HER CORPSE IN ONE OF THE NUMEROUS VAULTS IN THE DEPTHS OF THE BUILDING, FOR A TIME UNTIL THE FAMILY MAUSOLEUM COULD BE RE-ERECTED.
OH!
DON'T BE ALARMED, EDGAR. IT IS MERELY MY GRANDMOTHER, MARY ELLIANNE USHER. HER ROTTEN COFFIN WAS RUINED WHEN THE TOMB COLLAPSED. NOW SHE MUST WAIT FOR A NEW ONE.

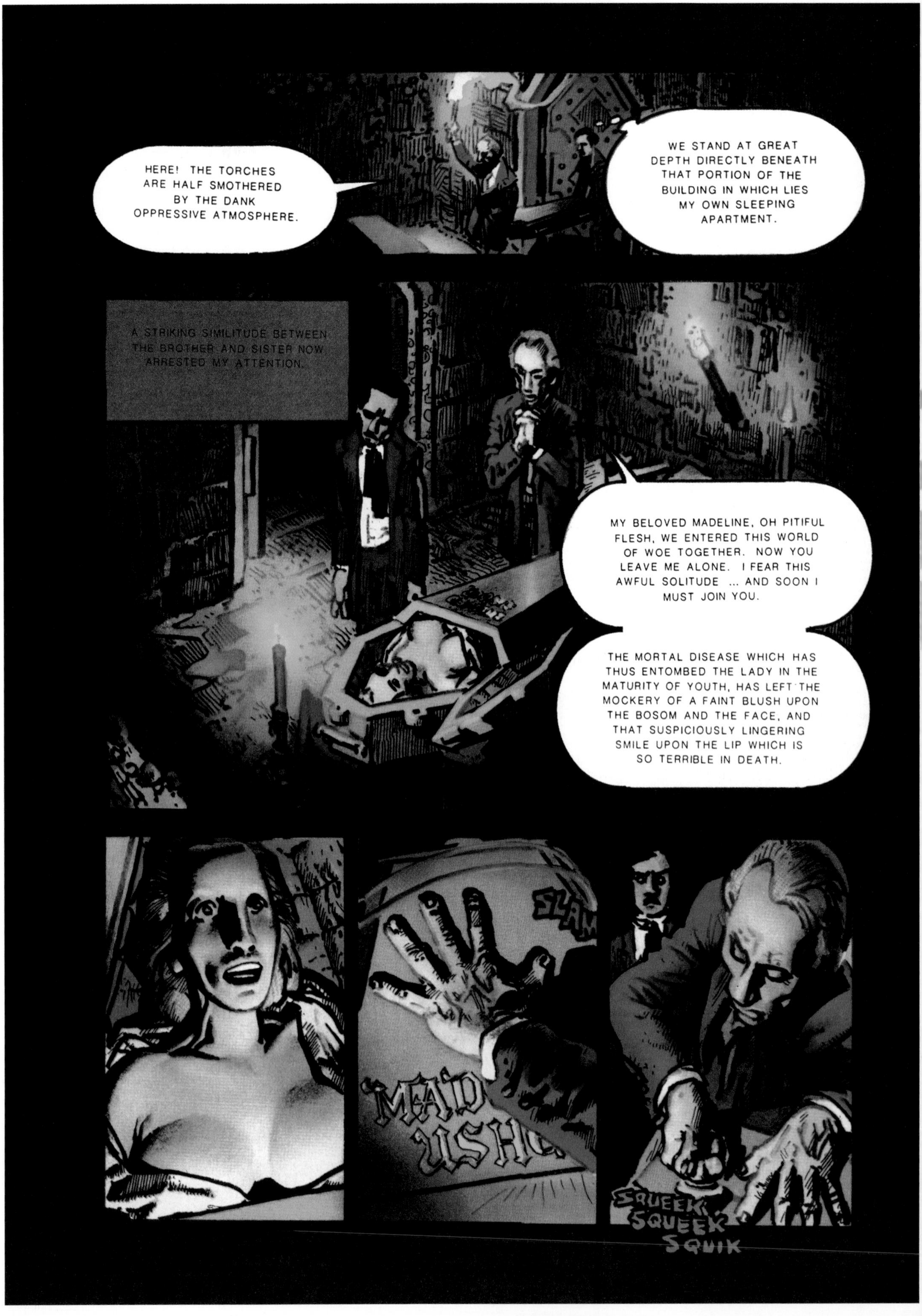
HERE! THE TORCHES ARE HALF SMOTHERED BY THE DANK OPPRESSIVE ATMOSPHERE.
WE STAND AT GREAT DEPTH DIRECTLY BENEATH THAT PORTION OF THE BUILDING IN WHICH LIES MY OWN SLEEPING APARTMENT.
A STRIKING SIMILITUDE BETWEEN THE BROTHER AND SISTER NOW ARRESTED MY ATTENTION.
MY BELOVED MADELINE, OH PITIFUL FLESH, WE ENTERED THIS WORLD OF WOE TOGETHER. NOW YOU LEAVE ME ALONE. I FEAR THIS AWFUL SOLITUDE ... AND SOON I MUST JOIN YOU.
THE MORTAL DISEASE WHICH HAS THUS ENTOMBED THE LADY IN THE MATURITY OF YOUTH, HAS LEFT THE MOCKERY OF A FAINT BLUSH UPON THE BOSOM AND THE FACE, AND THAT SUSPICIOUSLY LINGERING SMILE UPON THE LIP WHICH IS SO TERRIBLE IN DEATH.
SLAM
SQUEEK SQUEEK SQUIK

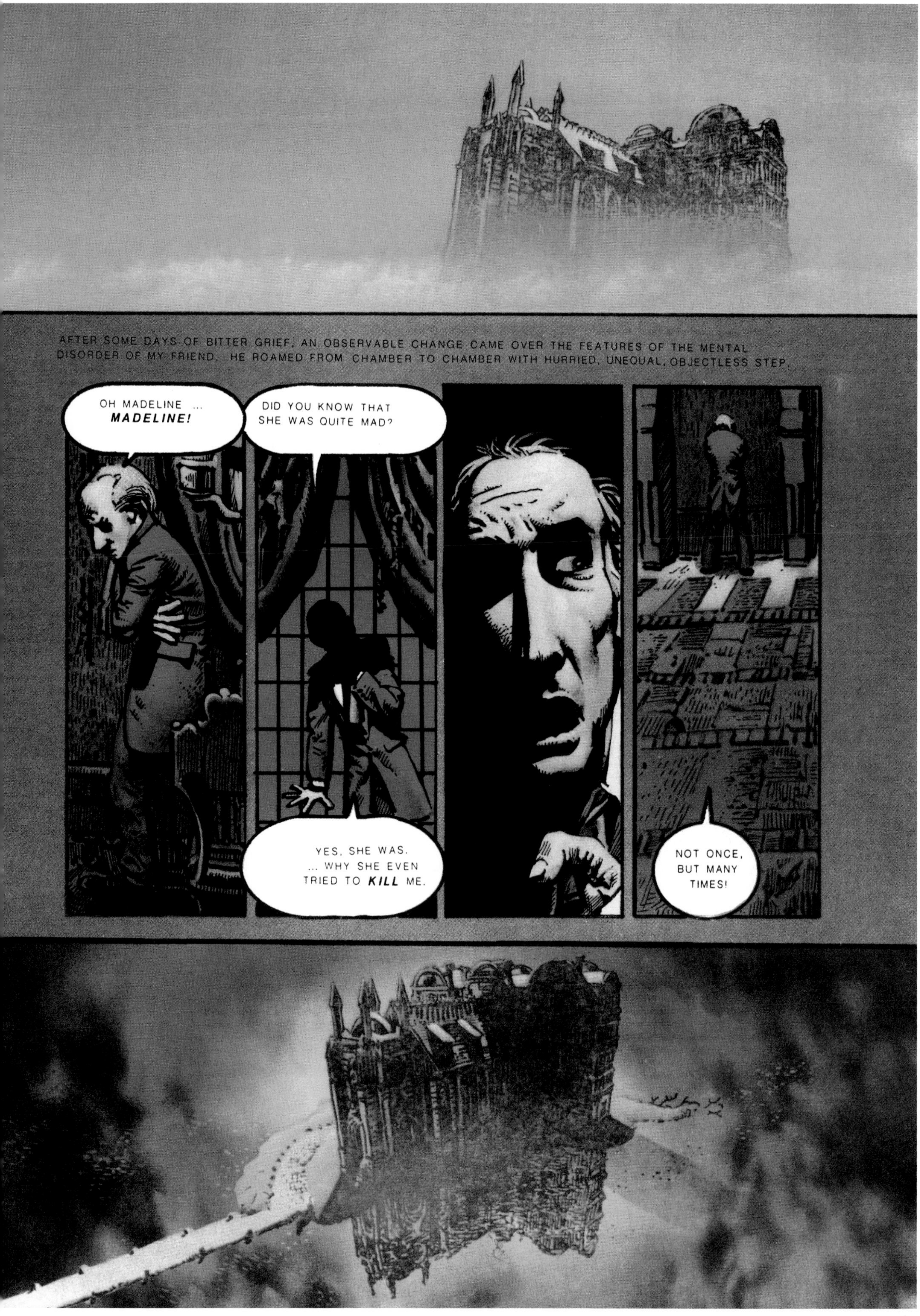

AFTER SOME DAYS OF BITTER GRIEF, AN OBSERVABLE CHANGE CAME OVER THE FEATURES OF THE MENTAL DISORDER OF MY FRIEND. HE ROAMED FROM CHAMBER TO CHAMBER WITH HURRIED, UNEQUAL, OBJECTLESS STEP.
OH MADELINE ... MADELINE!
DID YOU KNOW THAT SHE WAS QUITE MAD?
YES, SHE WAS. ... WHY SHE EVEN TRIED TO KILL ME.
NOT ONCE, BUT MANY TIMES!

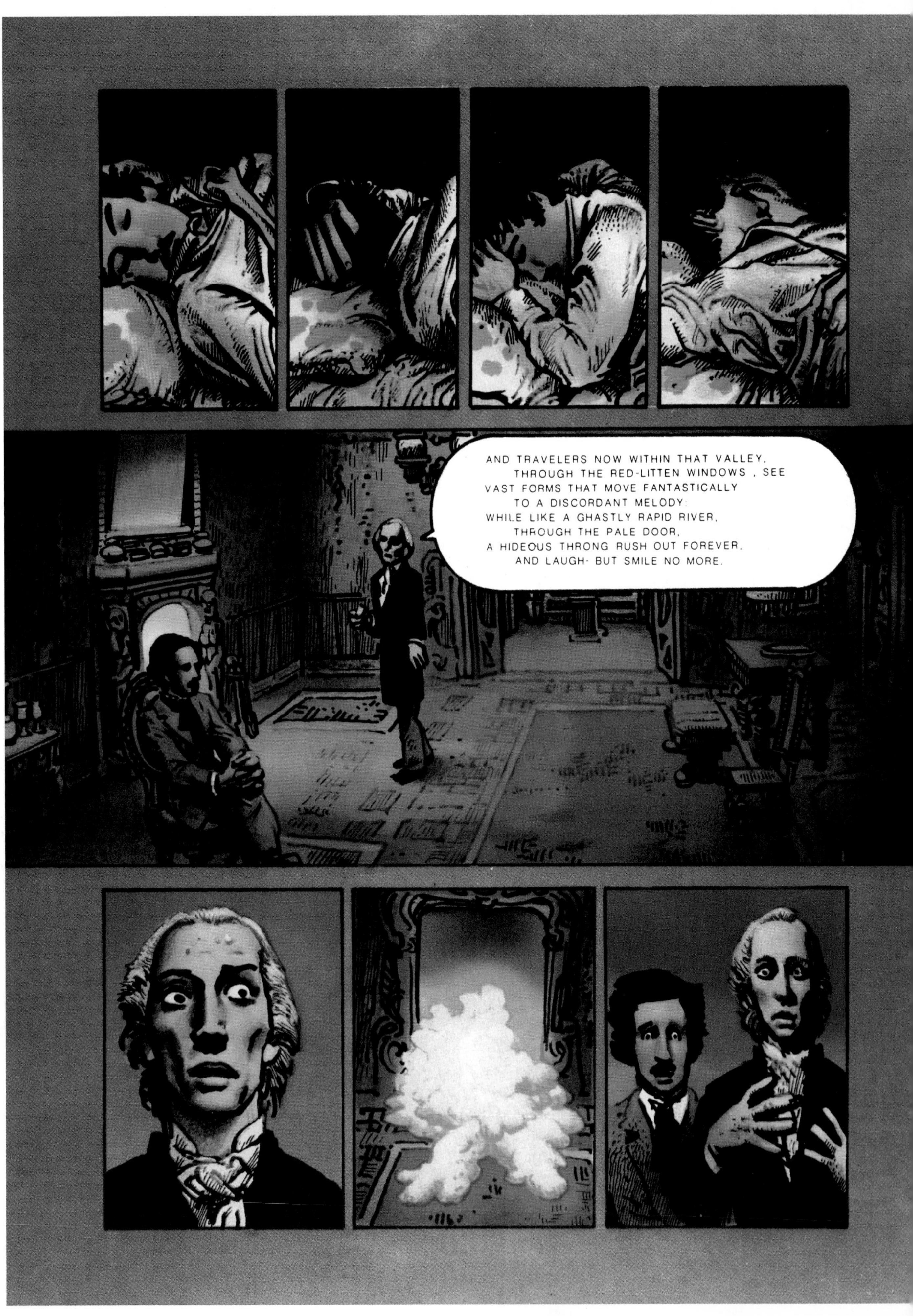
AND TRAVELERS NOW WITHIN THAT VALLEY,
THROUGH THE RED-LITTEN WINDOWS , SEE
VAST FORMS THAT MOVE FANTASTICALLY
TO A DISCORDANT MELODY:
WHILE LIKE A GHASTLY RAPID RIVER,
THROUGH THE PALE DOOR,
A HIDEOUS THRONG RUSH OUT FOREVER,
AND LAUGH- BUT SMILE NO MORE.

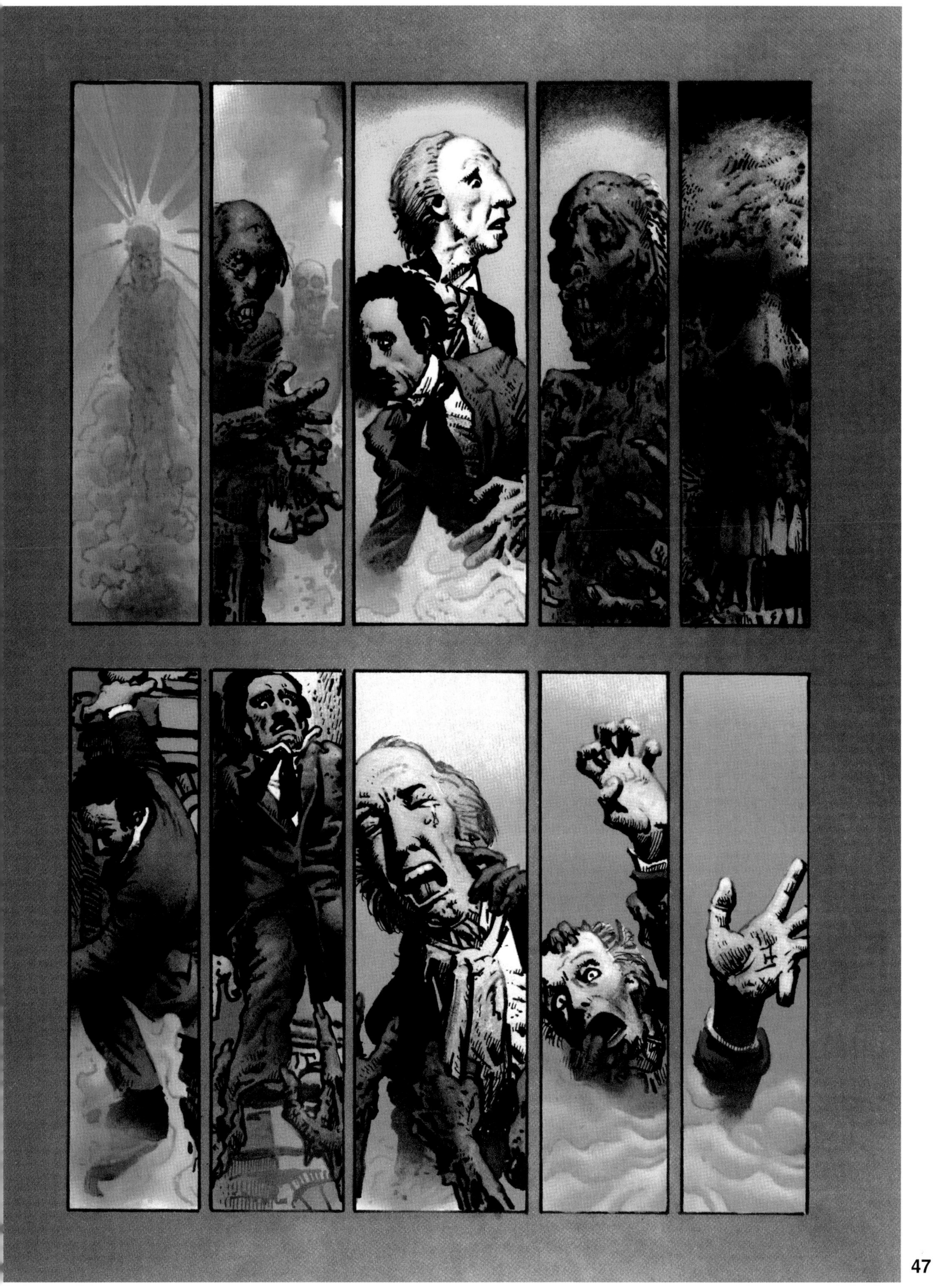

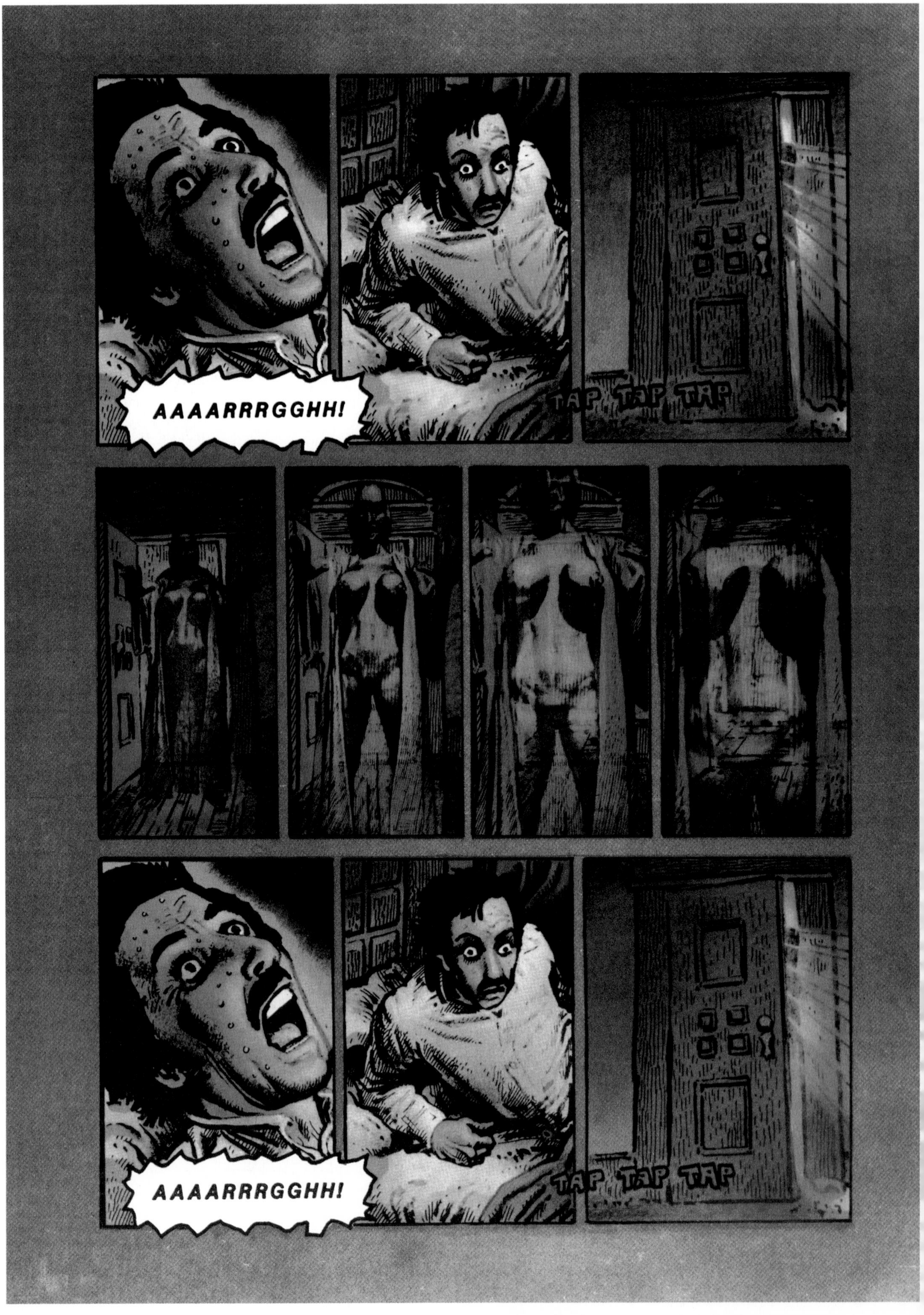
AAAARRRGGHH!
TAP TAP TAP
AAAARRRGGHH!
TAP TAP TAP

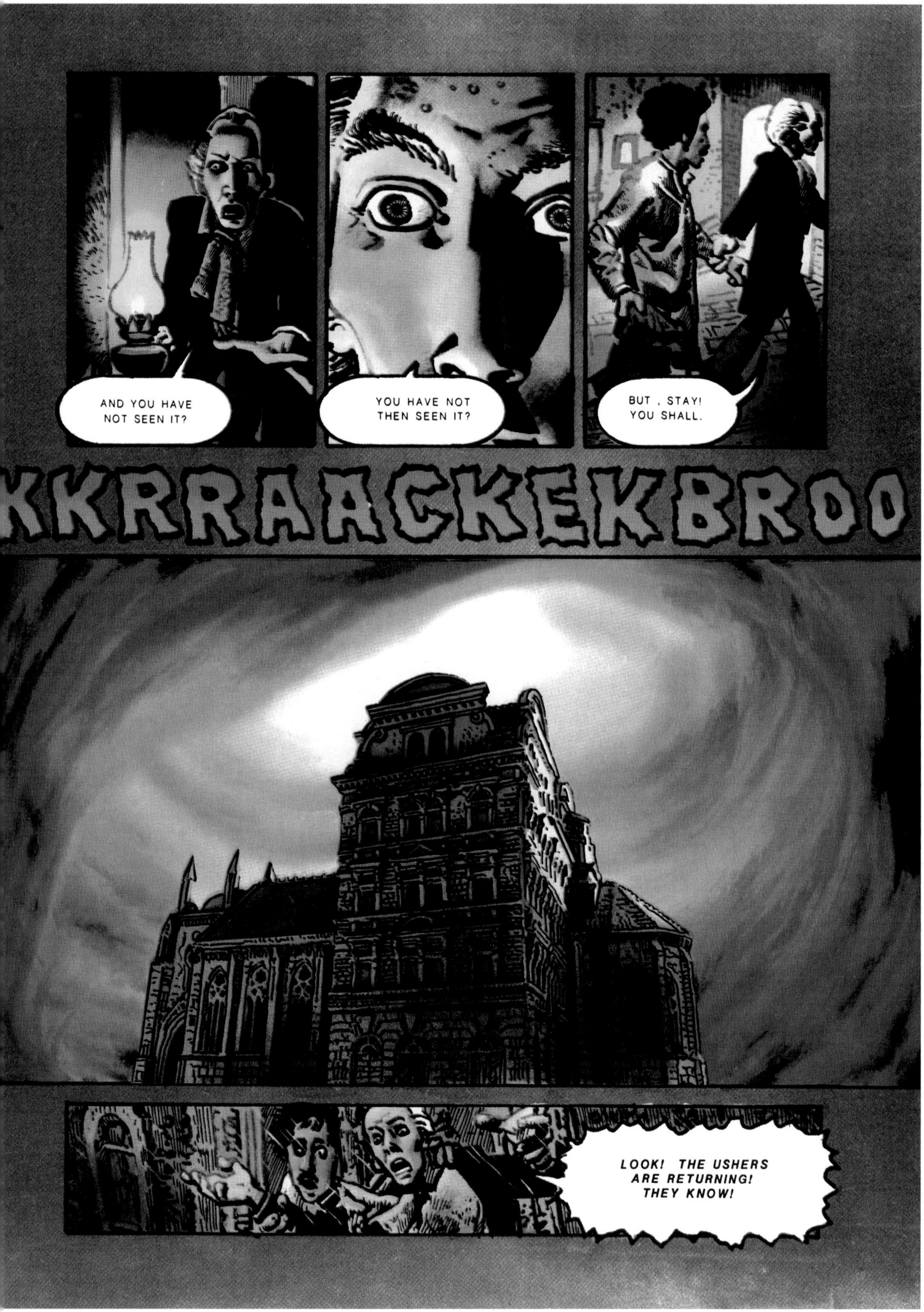
AND YOU HAVE NOT SEEN IT?
YOU HAVE NOT THEN SEEN IT?
BUT , STAY! YOU SHALL.
KKRRAACKEKBROO
LOOK! THE USHERS ARE RETURNING! THEY KNOW!

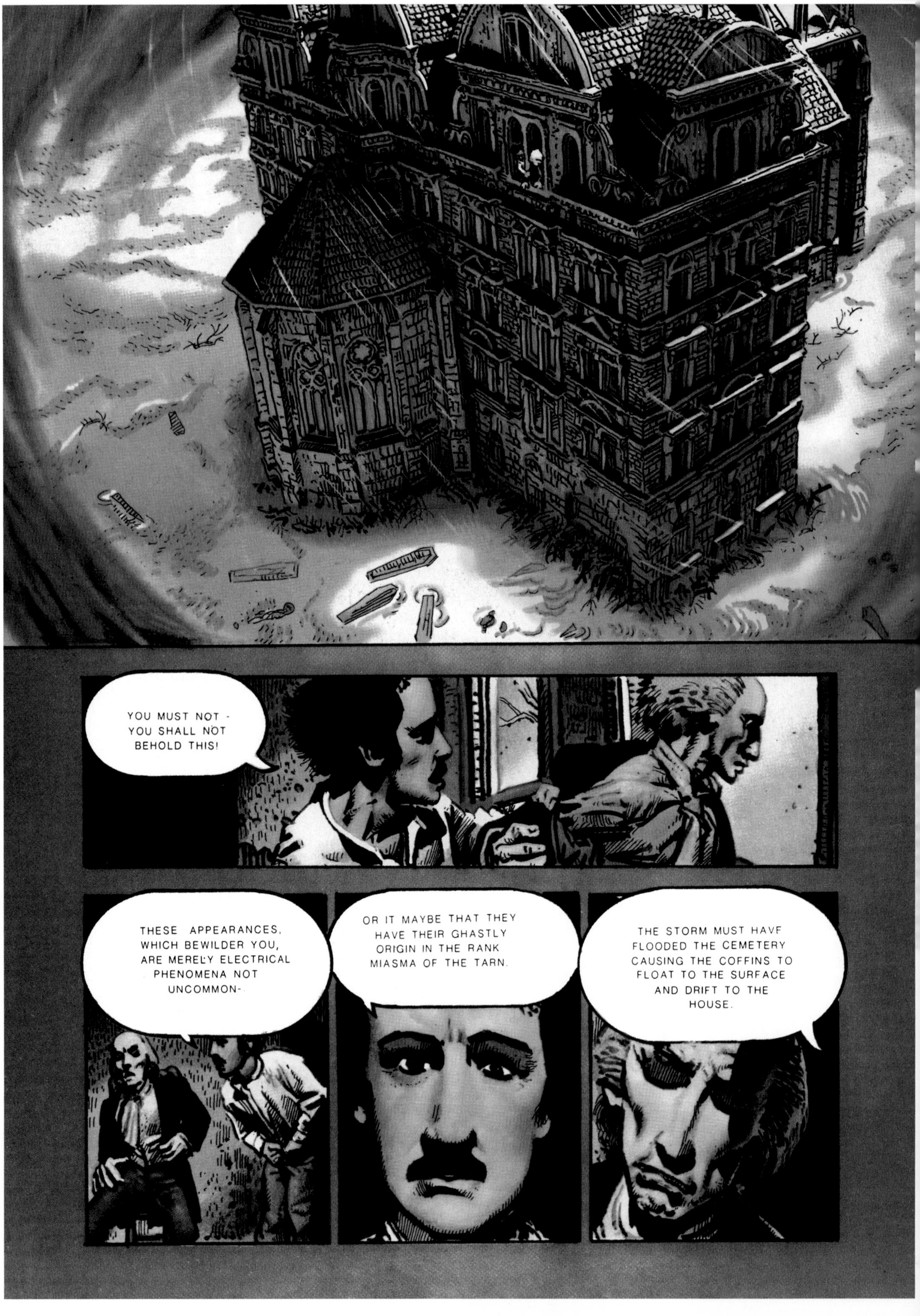
YOU MUST NOT - YOU SHALL NOT BEHOLD THIS!
THESE APPEARANCES, WHICH BEWILDER YOU, ARE MERELY ELECTRICAL PHENOMENA NOT UNCOMMON-.
OR IT MAYBE THAT THEY HAVE THEIR GHASTLY ORIGIN IN THE RANK MIASMA OF THE TARN.
THE STORM MUST HAVE FLOODED THE CEMETERY CAUSING THE COFFINS TO FLOAT TO THE SURFACE AND DRIFT TO THE HOUSE.

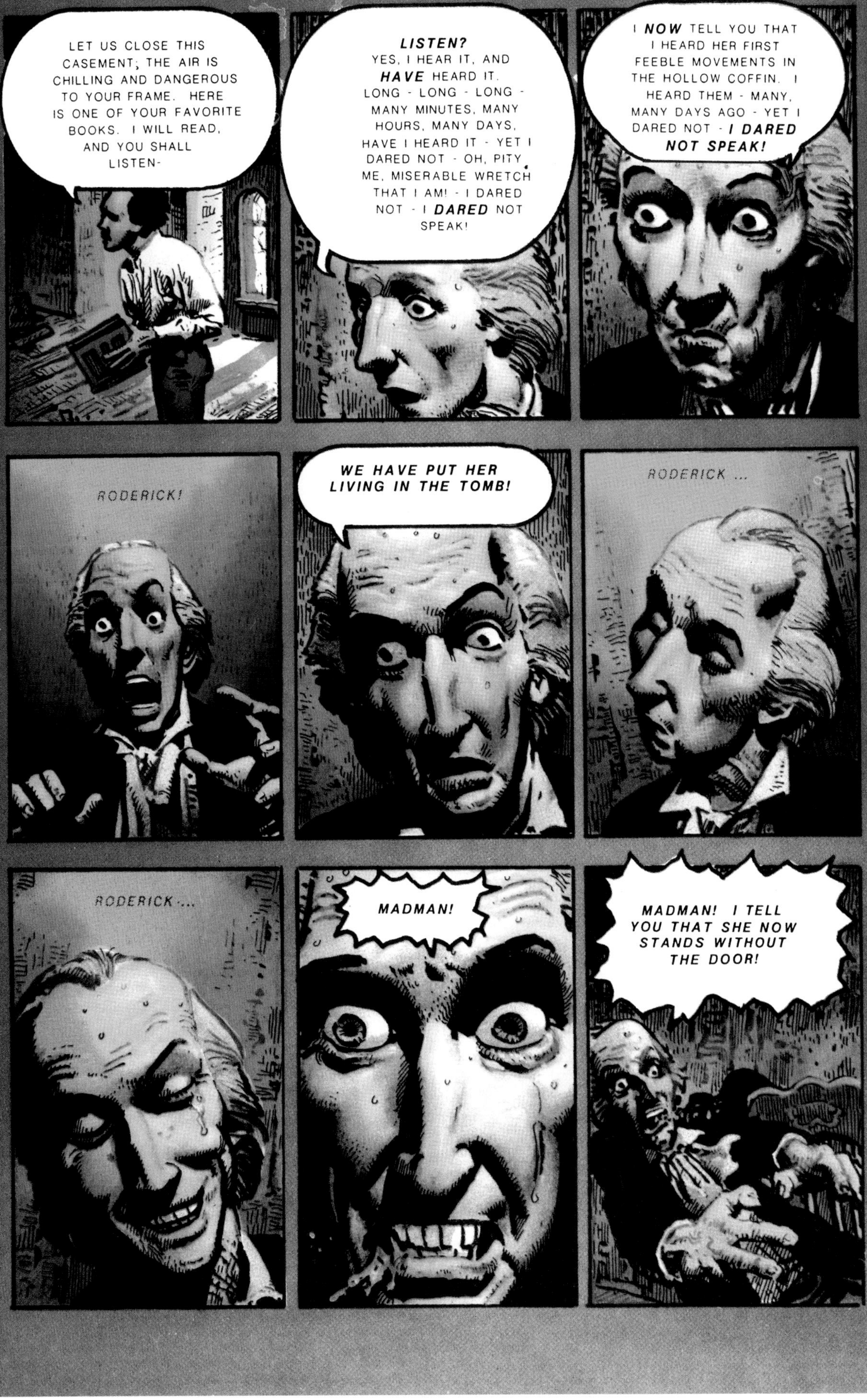
LET US CLOSE THIS CASEMENT; THE AIR IS CHILLING AND DANGEROUS TO YOUR FRAME. HERE IS ONE OF YOUR FAVORITE BOOKS. I WILL READ, AND YOU SHALL LISTEN-
LISTEN? YES, I HEAR IT, AND HAVE HEARD IT. LONG - LONG - LONG - MANY MINUTES, MANY HOURS, MANY DAYS, HAVE I HEARD IT - YET I DARED NOT - OH, PITY ME, MISERABLE WRETCH THAT I AM! - I DARED NOT - I DARED NOT SPEAK!
I NOW TELL YOU THAT I HEARD HER FIRST FEEBLE MOVEMENTS IN THE HOLLOW COFFIN. I HEARD THEM - MANY, MANY DAYS AGO - YET I DARED NOT - I DARED NOT SPEAK!
RODERICK!
WE HAVE PUT HER LIVING IN THE TOMB!
RODERICK ...
RODERICK ...
MADMAN!
MADMAN! I TELL YOU THAT SHE NOW STANDS WITHOUT THE DOOR!

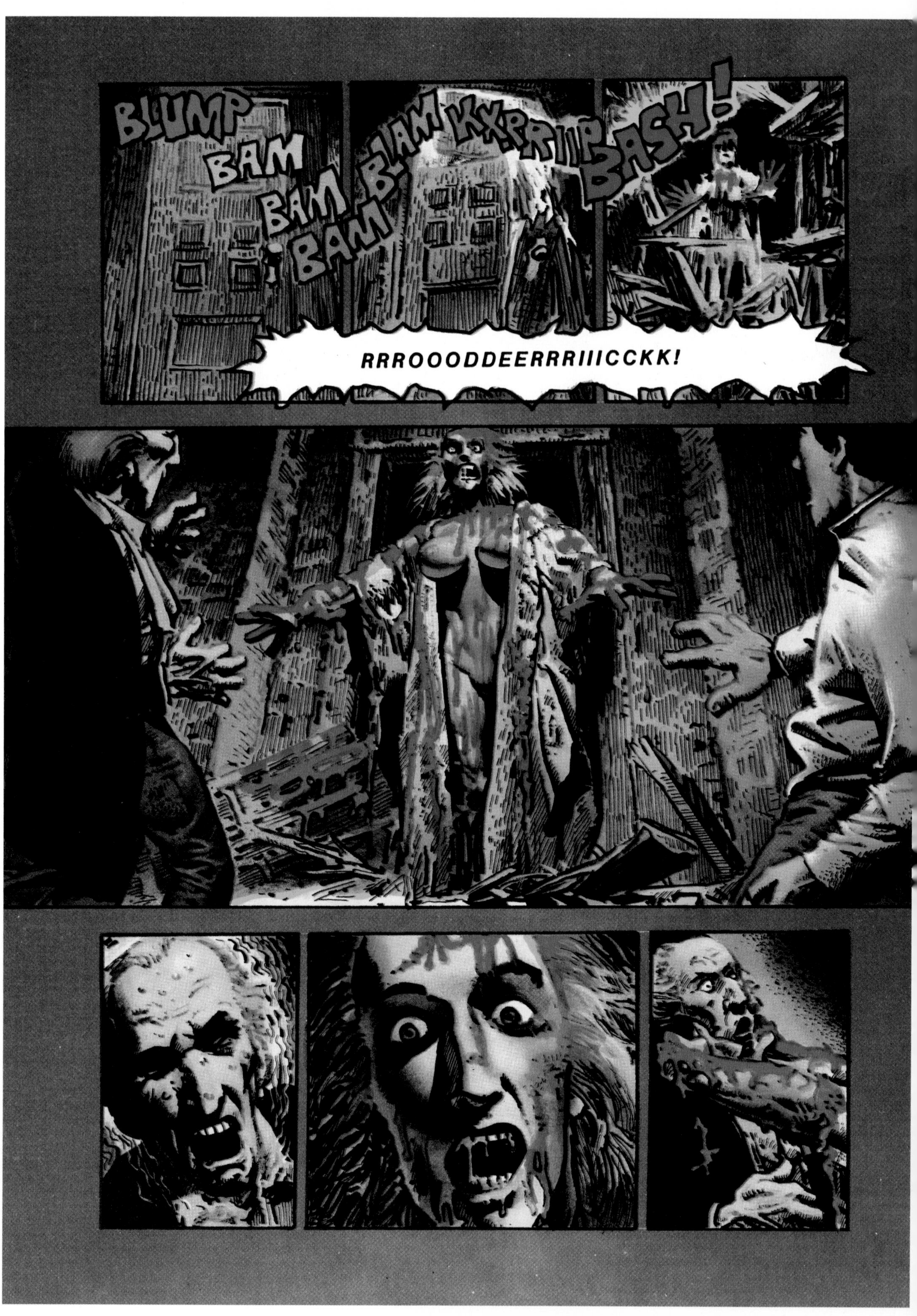
BLUMP
BAM
BAM
BAM
BLAM
BASH!
RRROOOODDEERRRRIIICCKK!

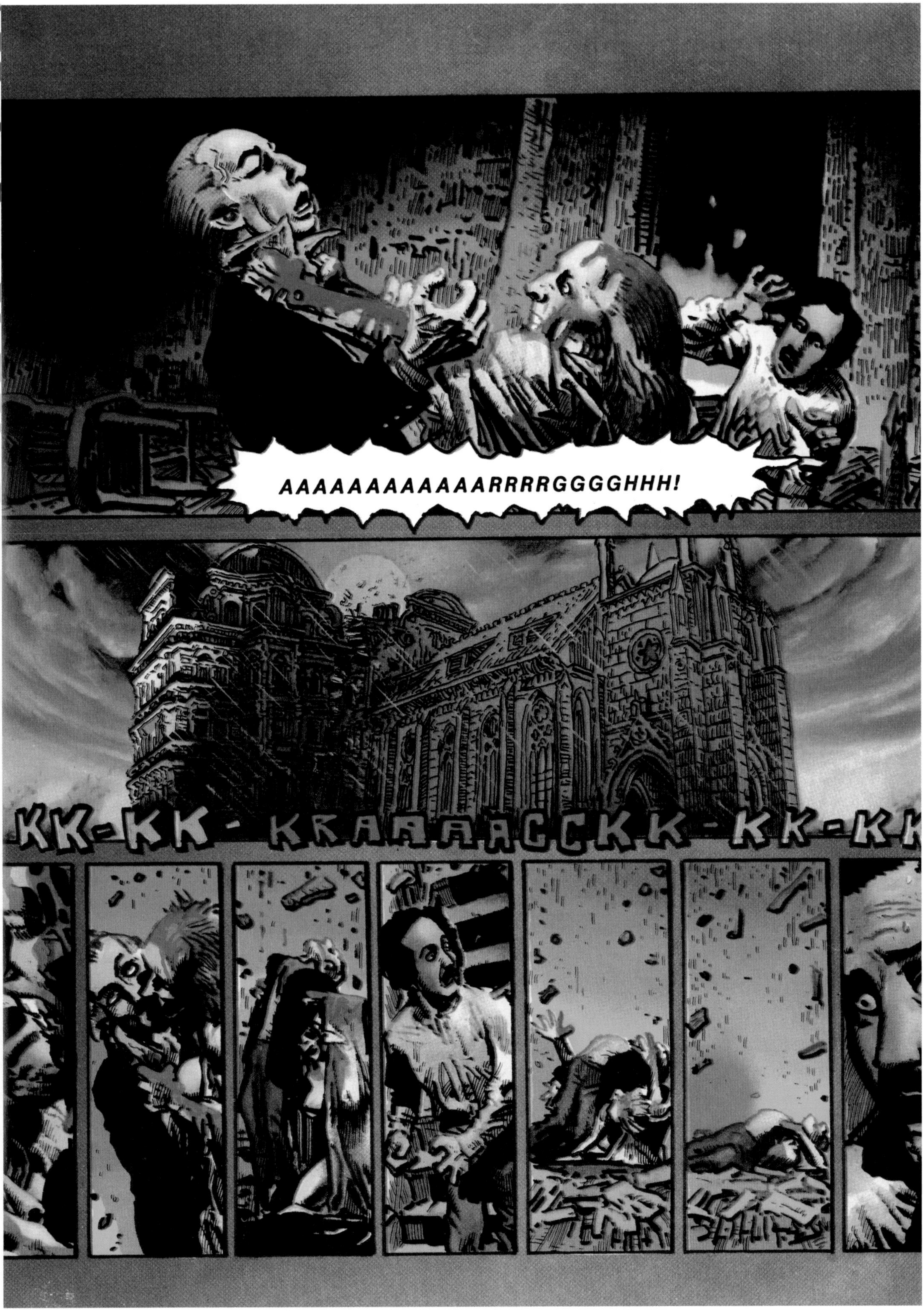
AAAAAAAAAAAARRRRGGGGHHH!
KK-KK-KRAAAAACCKK-KK-KK

KA - KKRRAASSHH!

MY BRAIN REELED AS I SAW THE MIGHTY WALLS RUSHING ASUNDER - THERE WAS A LONG TUMULTUOUS SOUND LIKE THE VOICE OF A THOUSAND WATERS - AND THE DEEP AND DANK TARN AT MY FEET CLOSED SULLENLY AND SILENTLY OVER THE FRAGMENTS OF THE **HOUSE OF USHER.**

THE END

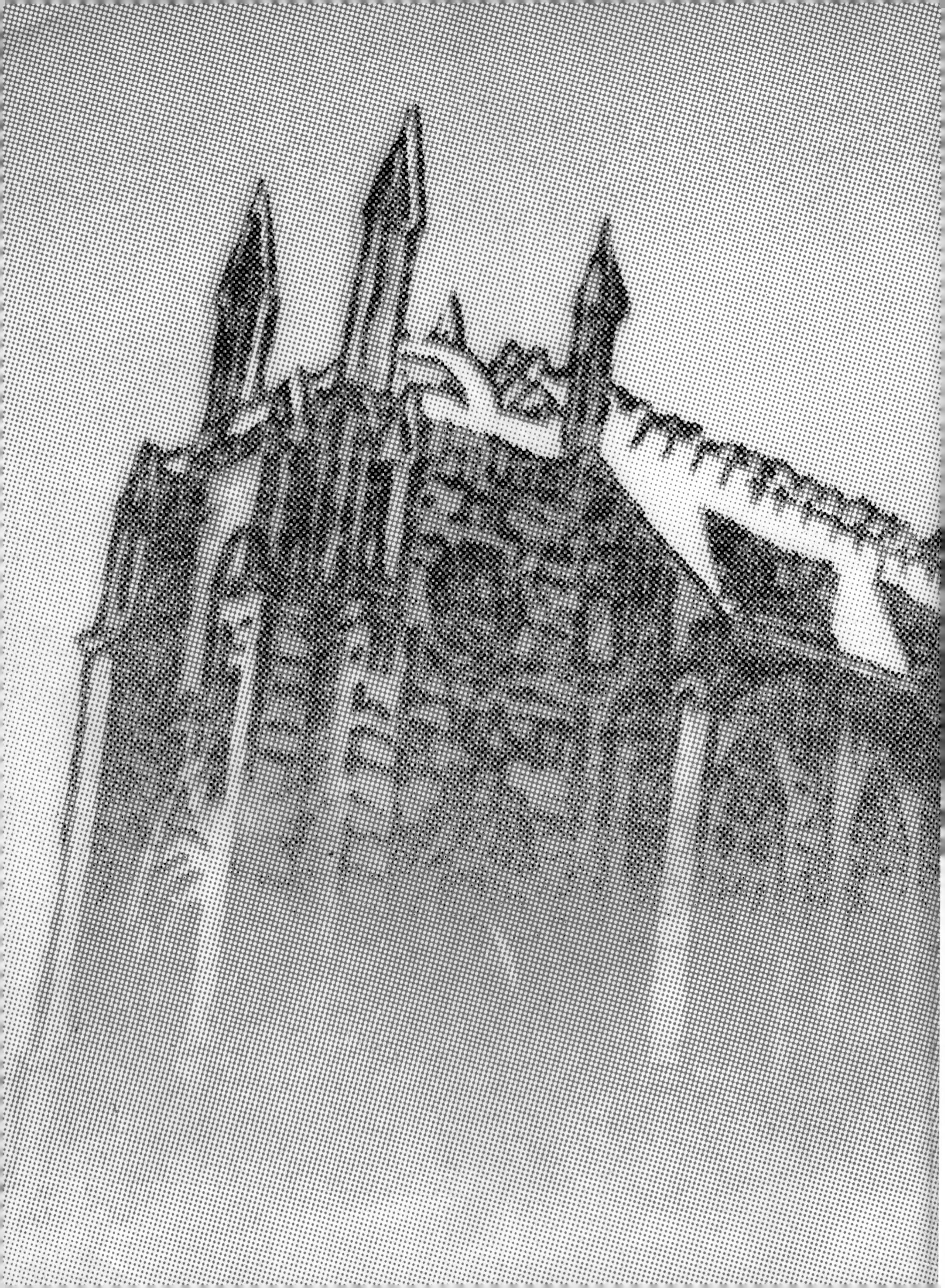

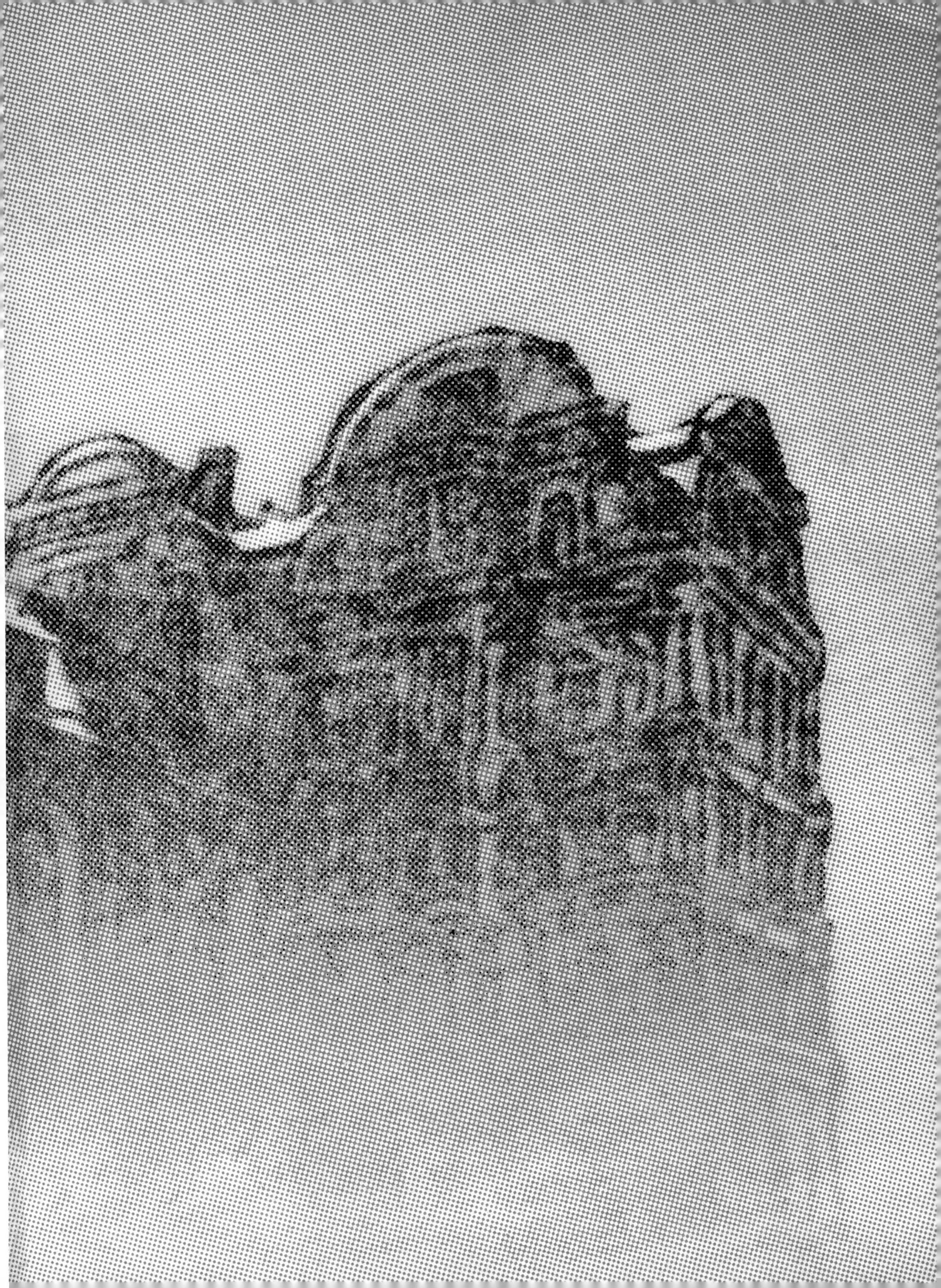